OUTRAGEOUS SUGGESTION

A woman thinks her plot to murder her husband is foolproof — but it will set off ricocheting complications. When a stranger calls at an old inn during a vicious storm, the elderly resident and her manservant concoct a sinister plan. A travelling salesman picks up a secretly dangerous hitch-hiker. A woman telephones a private detective agency and hangs up abruptly, piquing the curiosity of the investigator. And a knife thrower's assistant is murdered — but is her jealous partner responsible?

ERNEST DUDLEY

OUTRAGEOUS SUGGESTION
& OTHER STORIES

Complete and Unabridged

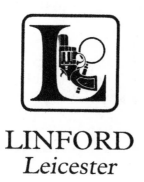

LINFORD
Leicester

First published in Great Britain

First Linford Edition
published 2018

A catalogue record for this book is available
from the British Library.

ISBN 978–1–4448–3919–7

Published by
F. A. Thorpe (Publishing)
Anstey, Leicestershire

Set by Words & Graphics Ltd.
Anstey, Leicestershire
Printed and bound in Great Britain by
T. J. International Ltd., Padstow, Cornwall

This book is printed on acid-free paper

Contents

Outrageous Suggestion

Novelized by Philip Harbottle
from the play by Ernest Dudley

1

Freda Nutting, small-time actress and model, was sitting alone in the living room of her home reading, and listening to music from her transistor radio. The room was not luxurious, but it was comfortably furnished, albeit rather untidy. It was a late summer evening, and the curtains were drawn.

A clock chimed six, and Freda looked up from her book, her manner apprehensive.

She checked the time on her watch, then switched off the radio, and stood up. Crossing to the curtained window, she parted the curtains a little and peeped out.

She watched for a second or two, then nodded imperceptibly, as if satisfied about something she had seen. She picked up the telephone on the desk adjacent to the window, and dialled a local number.

A man's voice answered her almost immediately.

'Is this the young man I spoke to last night?' Freda asked. 'On what number . . . ? Correct. Can you hear me distinctly . . . ? Good . . . '

She peeped again between the curtains.

' . . . Opposite the box where you are, are some flats. I am speaking from number five, ground floor . . . I'll give you a light signal so you'll know which it is . . . '

Putting down the receiver carefully, Freda crossed to the light switch, put the main lights out and then on again, and returned to the desk and picked up the phone.

'O.K.?' Freda resumed. 'Our gardens have back gates in the narrow lane. Go to number five. I have left the key on the wall just under the ivy . . . Bring it with you. Come through the garden, up the stone stairs, and let yourself in. No one must see you. All right . . . ?'

After hanging up the phone, Freda remained standing by the desk for a few moments, deep in thought. Picking up a cigarette and lighter from the desk, she took a deep drag, as might one who faces a nervous ordeal.

Seating herself in the desk chair she waited, her eye on the garden window.

After a moment a young man cautiously let himself in.

He was tough-looking, well-made, with an animal charm that seemed oddly professional. His face broke into a smile as he saw she was awaiting him. He did not shut the garden window behind him, but stood looking around the room warily. Then he faced her, playing with a key still in his hand.

They stood looking at each other for a few seconds, then Freda said: 'We are alone and we shall not be disturbed.'

'That's all right then.'

'What is your name?' Freda demanded.

'Vic, madam.'

'Same as your telephone exchange!' Freda said sharply. 'Coincidence?'

'Convenience.' Vic smiled faintly.

'I am Mrs. Howard Nutting,' Freda informed him.

'Pleased to meet you, Mrs. Nutting.'

5

'What do you do for a living?'

The man shrugged. 'You saw my card in the window. Must have, or you couldn't have called me.'

Freda took a sheet of notepaper from her pocket, and read from it:

'"Fit young man. Jobs about the house. Anything legal. Victoria 4249, Thursdays, seven to eight p.m."' She gave him a sharp look. 'Victoria 4249 is a public call box. Why do you use a *public* telephone?'

The man shrugged. 'Can't afford a *private* one.'

Freda looked at him shrewdly. 'The kind of contacts you are after are more likely to be made over the telephone . . . than put into writing, I mean?'

His eyes narrowed defensively. 'Some people can't write, madam . . . '

Freda smiled faintly. 'Some may not wish to.'

'Yourself, for instance?' he challenged.

'Myself, for instance,' she assented frankly. 'So, each Thursday evening, you wait by your box; and if there is a call, you answer it?'

'Clever girl!'

6

'As you did last night when *I* called.'

He nodded. 'Uh-huh.'

'I saw you. I was calling from the box next to yours.' Freda paused, then added: 'Yours had 'Out of order' chalked on the door. Clever boy!'

The man smiled. 'You've gone to a lot of hush-hush to get me here, Mrs. Nutting; what for, exactly?'

'A 'job about the house',' she answered blandly.

He gave a cynical smile. 'I get the impression it's not the washing-up!'

'And I get the impression you don't expect it to be.'

'What do you want me for, Mrs. Nutting?'

Freda stubbed out her cigarette in the ash tray on the desk. 'Don't rush me.' She looked at him appraisingly. 'Do *many* people phone you?'

'Enough.'

'Women, I'd guess. Your little card seemed worded to appeal to women.'

''Jobs about the house' is *their* department, madam.' He spread his hands.

'And what do they ask you to do?'
Freda pursued.

'Carpet-cleaning, floor-polishing, window-washing, dog-trotting . . . '

'All depressingly legal!'

'I state on my card, madam,' he said cautiously, ' "anything legal".'

'Which means,' Freda said shrewdly, 'illegal preferred if better-paid and not too dangerous. Otherwise, why put it?'

'You think so?' He was still being cautious.

'I hope so, because it was *that* which decided me . . . to call you,' she admitted frankly. 'But I should hate to corrupt . . . honest industry.'

She watched as a variety of expressions crossed his face. Clearly he was struggling to size her up.

'Are you never asked to do *il*legal things, Vic?'

'Sometimes.' He was still guarded.

'What sort of things . . . Love-making?'

'Love-making is not illegal, madam.'

'Isn't it?' Freda smiled cynically. 'They always seem to be trying to stop it.' She paused, then added: 'Perhaps that's because it's a pleasure.'

'It's not always a pleasure,' he countered.

Freda considered him for a moment, then rose and put a hand in her pocket. Pulling out a pound note, she went over to him and offered him the money.

'Sorry I've troubled you.'

He made no move to accept the money. 'You've been no trouble.'

Freda waved the note invitingly. 'Forget it all the same.'

'Can you tell me why you got me here?'

'It would be a waste of time.' Freda was turning away when the man suddenly grabbed the note.

'I'm not short of *time*.' He tucked the money into his top pocket.

She looked at him for a second, then smiled and came to a decision.

Moving over to the sideboard drawer, she took out a pair of cotton gloves and a duster. Turning back to him, she handed him the gloves.

'Put these on,' she commanded. 'Touch nothing in this room without them on.' She held out a hand. 'Give me that key.'

Taking the key from him, she wiped it carefully in the duster, and put it in a little jug on the sideboard. Then, crossing to the garden window, Freda wiped the handles which he had touched. She closed the window, bolting it.

Replacing the duster in the sideboard drawer, she went back to her chair at the desk, and sat down again, turning the chair to face him directly.

Watching her narrowly, he donned the gloves as she had directed.

'Pity we don't live in the Middle Ages, isn't it?' Freda remarked. 'Their services, in some respects, were more imaginative than ours.'

'I should have said more primitive . . . '

'They had primitive problems for which they found primitive solutions,' Freda said. 'We have the same problems, but are not allowed the same solutions.'

Vic shrugged. 'The Welfare State has its limitations.'

'If I were Elizabeth the First, you would climb the steps of my throne and I would whisper in your ear and away you would go. Later you would come back and whisper in my ear. And I would smile and give you gold.' Freda smiled, and paused. 'So simple! And I wouldn't even see any blood.'

The man tensed. 'Blood, Mrs. Nutting? Whose?'

'My husband's.'

Vic tightened his lips, and began to take off the gloves. 'I'm an absolute cad to refuse, of course, but . . . '

'You are not going to refuse,' Freda interrupted him.

He paused in the discarding of the gloves.

'You know why?' Freda hurried on. 'Because it's the easiest 'job about the house' you'll ever get. Ten times easier than satisfying a middle-aged woman . . . and a hundred times better-paid. You just add two noughts.'

His smiled thoughtfully.

'You like money?' Freda asked.

'Mad about it. But mad about my liberty, too.'

'Your liberty would be in no danger,' she assured him.

He hesitated, then: 'What makes the

job so easy, Mrs. Nutting?'

'Bring that hard chair forward and sit on it.' She pointed to a chair across the room.

When he had complied, Freda went on earnestly: 'The job is easy because the victim himself has done all the ground-work, leaving us ... merely ... to complete things.'

'How come?'

'He has supplied the *reason* for his murder ... money in the house; *and* also created the extreme *likelihood* of his murder ... certain young men with criminal records know the money is here.'

Vic frowned. 'I don't understand. Who are these young men?'

'They are guests at a holiday camp, on the coast of Sussex, run by my husband. Only a tiny place; little more than a collection of huts left by the Army ... '

'Uh-huh. Go on ... '

'My husband's brother, a do-gooder, bought the place cheap. The idea being that lads coming out of approved schools could go there for a while. Some of them, you see, have no homes, or are unwanted there . . . '

Vic furrowed his brow. 'This brother might be a — '

Freda smiled and waved a hand. 'He won't — he's dead! He got drowned and my husband inherited the place, using it himself sometimes to relax from writing. He comes back tomorrow after two weeks there. He'll bring the money with him.'

'What money is it?'

'Proceeds from Bingo sessions and talent contests organised by the boys. The camp has to be self-supporting, you see.'

'So the boys know about the money?' Vic was thoughtful.

Freda nodded. 'And it's the one thing they're always short of. That's why the job is a pushover.'

'Why does he bring the money home?'

'To take to the bank. There's no bank down there. He comes up tomorrow for a dinner at the Connaught Rooms. An annual do he never misses.'

'I see . . . What sort of money will it be?'

'Might be a hundred or so.' Freda

raised her eyebrows. 'Does it matter?'

'A man doesn't commit murder for just a hundred or so,' Vic demurred.

Freda shook her head. 'One of *those* boys would. And that will be my story to the police.'

'What are *you* offering?' he asked bluntly.

'Five hundred,' Freda answered promptly. 'A hundred now, and the rest when the job is done.'

'*And* the Bingo money?'

'That as well, naturally,' Freda conceded. '*That* is the reason for the murder.'

Vic rose from his chair and moved about thoughtfully. Finding himself near Howard's picture standing on the sideboard, he studied it.

'This him?'

'Yes. It's a recent photo.'

He pulled on the gloves again, and picked up the picture.

'How old is he?'

'Thirty-five.'

'And what does he do? Besides this camp lark?'

'The camp is something that's been

dumped on him. His living is writing
. . . for films, chiefly.'

'Uh-huh. Describe him . . . physical
appearance.'

'Five foot eight, slight build . . .
Howard's a fairly small man. You
wouldn't find him . . . any trouble . . . '

Replacing the picture, he glanced about
him. 'Just the two of you live here?'

'Yes.'

'You work too?' He looked at her
appraisingly. 'You look the professional
type.'

Freda smiled faintly. 'I do a bit of
acting and modelling. I'm not entirely
dependent on my husband, if that's what
you're wondering.'

'Has he any relations?'

'Not now. There was only the brother
. . . who was drowned.'

'So that means . . . everything . . .
would come to you?'

'True. But in my husband's case, that's
not very much.'

Vic had more questions: 'What are his
hobbies?'

'Spot of cooking sometimes. Makes

curries . . . stinks the place out. Photography . . . nothing serious.'

'Men friends?'

'Just a few writing types.' Freda snorted. 'I find them boring as hell.'

'Do they come here?'

'Not often, thank God! Put paid to a bottle of gin the last time.'

'Female friends?'

Freda shook her head slowly. 'He's . . . unattractive, physically. An intellectual, too. I'd say . . . no female friends.'

'Not even yourself?'

'You can say that again!'

Vic glanced round the room again. 'What's the set-up here?'

Freda rose and went over to Howard's bedroom and threw open the door for the man to see in.

'That's his bedroom. Also serves as an office, as you can see.'

After looking in, Vic followed her to her own bedroom. She opened the door and he looked in briefly.

'This one's mine. We no longer live as man and wife. We meet, when he's here, at mealtimes. In the evening he works, or goes to his club. Me? I'm not short of friends.'

They drifted back into the lounge. Vic went over to the picture and looked at it again.

'Well?' Freda said impatiently. 'Will you do it?'

He replaced the picture, and deliberated. Then: 'It's very specialised work, Mrs. Nutting . . . '

'Five hundred is all I can offer,' Freda said quickly. 'It's all I've got.'

'I'd be taking a big risk . . . '

'So would I!' She looked at him indignantly. 'Parting with my life savings — '

'You don't part with those until he's dead,' he pointed out. 'Then you collect *his*.'

'He might leave me debts, not savings. The price is five hundred, Vic, plus the Bingo money. It's not bad . . . tax-free at that.' Freda looked at him directly. 'Well, is it 'Yes' or 'No'?'

'When do you want this done?' he asked.

'Tomorrow night at seven.' Freda's eyes

gleamed. 'Everything is in our favour then. Being Monday, it's my regular night out. That gives me my alibi. Also, we know his movements. He'll be getting ready to go to his dinner at the Connaught Rooms. And the money will be here. He will have brought it with him.'

'All right. Now tell me your plan.'

'First, the layout of these flats . . . ' She waved a hand excitedly. 'There's the front entrance, guarded by Ernie the porter. Back gate, Yale lock, you know about that.'

He nodded, his eyes following her as she went over to the garden window.

'This garden window . . . is secured with a single bolt.' She demonstrated its action, and turned back to look at him. 'Then, most important, the side door . . . '

'The one down the steps where the dustbins are?'

'You've seen it?'

'From the pavement.'

'Good!' She nodded in satisfaction. 'It has no lock but a bolt. The boilerman secures it when he finishes at five. He opens up again next morning at eight. People with business here between those times use the front entrance.'

'Do the tenants go to the dustbins at night?'

'No. The dailies see to such things each morning.'

'Carry on,' he invited gravely.

'Tomorrow evening, I shall leave here at six-thirty. Last thing before I go, I shall pop down to the dustbins to empty — ' She pointed to the paper bin. ' — this. I shall unbolt the door for you. On my way out, I shall ask the porter to get my husband on the buzzer here.' She indicated it on the wall to the right of the fireplace. 'I'll tell him I think I've left the gas on. This will prove my husband was alive when I left.'

'I see. Then?'

'I call a cab. I go to my club. It's a tiny theatre club in Rickmore Street. There I shall have a drink and a natter with an old friend, Lucy. The club is very quiet. We shall sit *near the telephone box.*'

'I get you. Go on.'

19

'At seven o'clock you come to the side door, let yourself in, and bolt the door after you. Have a torch, don't switch on any light, and don't make any noise. Come along the passageway, ignoring the door on your right — the boiler room — up the stone stairs, and you will find yourself in . . . ' She pointed to the hall door. ' . . . this corridor . . . come, I'll show you.'

He followed her as she crossed to the hall door.

'Make sure the coast is clear first,' Freda said, opening the door and then signalling for him to join her. He did so, standing just outside the door. He nodded as she pointed down the corridor, then stepped back as she closed the door.

'All right?'

'Yes.'

'I shall have told my husband that I have reported a fault on the telephone,' Freda elaborated. 'A noisy line, so he won't be surprised when he finds an . . . 'engineer' . . . at the door.'

Vic nodded. 'I take it I am the 'engineer'?'

'Yes. You must look the part: wear overalls and shoes which you will destroy later.' She paused, considering. 'Can you bring an old tool-bag?'

'No problem.'

'Right. In it you will have spare shoes and a paper carrier bag. Wear gloves, and don't take them off.'

She turned again to the hall door.

'You come to this door. You ring the bell. He . . . will answer it.'

'What if somebody else does?'

'They can't.' Freda shook her head emphatically. 'There will be nobody else here. Now! At the point where you ring the bell, you will be all keyed up and ready. Because as soon as you are in and the door shut, you are going to do it . . . instantly.'

Vic frowned his puzzlement. 'What's the hurry?'

'There are two important reasons for this,' Freda explained. 'First, have no conversation with him. It would weaken your resolve. Also . . . ' She indicated a decorative metal figure on a small table near where she was standing. ' . . . the murder weapon is right to your hand.'

Picking up a cushion from the settee facing the fireplace, she demonstrated for him.

'Tool-bag . . . in left hand . . . your right hand . . . free. While he is closing the door, you put down your bag, a perfectly natural action as if you were going to take off your gloves. Having closed the door, he must turn to show you . . . ' She pointed to the desk. ' . . . where the phone is. You reach out . . . ' She demonstrated, using the metal figure. ' . . . the whole thing is done in one movement.'

She replaced the metal figure.

He picked it up, trying the feel of it. 'Pretty heavy,' he commented.

'Good grip? Not likely to break?'

As he tried it for weight and grip, Freda said: 'Try the movement.'

Throwing him the cushion, she pretended that she had just admitted him and was closing the door.

He replaced the metal figure, then taking the cushion he went to the same point that she had, and put it down with his left hand.

'Telephone?' Freda pantomimed. 'Over there.'

She had her back to him. He grabbed the figure and made the movement of striking.

Freda turned, smiling grimly. 'Simple, isn't it?'

'Uh-huh.' He replaced the figure. 'Very straightforward.'

'Your overalls and shoes will take care of any splashing,' Freda went on coldly. 'The job done, put them in the paper carrier, and take them out of the building with you. Destroy them later.'

'O.K.'

Freda replaced the cushion, and turned to him. 'Right. He's dead. You now send me a signal, letting me know you've done the deed.'

'How do I do that?'

'Simple.' She picked up her handbag and withdrew her small address book. 'Pick up the phone and dial . . . this number.' She showed him the number in her book, and waited whilst he wrote it down on his cigarette packet.

'The number of your club?'

Freda nodded. 'I shall answer, merely saying the number. You will tap your mouthpiece twice, once, twice again, and we will both hang up. O.K.?'

'O.K.,' he assented.

Getting herself a pair of gloves, Freda carefully put them on. 'By the way, the burglar was thirsty.' She reached for a tumbler from the sideboard, holding it carefully by the rim. 'I stole this glass from Victoria Coach Station.' She indicated a bottle of Coca-Cola. 'A man had just had Coca-Cola in it. He's bound to have left a nice set of fingerprints.'

'Not the sort of man with a set to match at Scotland Yard, I hope,' Vic remarked, smiling slightly.

'He was all in black, his luggage labelled 'College of Theology' somewhere,' Freda informed him as she put the glass and bottle away again. 'It will prove somebody was here, and give the police a lead. The fact that it leads nowhere, they won't find out till they get there. But all that is *my* department.'

She stepped nearer to him. 'Happy?'

'Yeah.' He sounded somewhat reluctant.

'You're worried about something.'

'No, no,' he assured her. 'Carry on.'

Freda took a breath, then: 'Then now comes the bit you won't like. Having done the job, and sent the signal, you have a two-hour wait . . . till I get here at nine.'

'Do you mind . . . ?'

'I want medical evidence that he died two hours before I found him,' Freda said firmly. 'That will be my alibi.'

'I'm to sit here *looking* at him for two hours? Worse! He may be looking at *me*!'

'Don't be morbid! Throw that rug over him . . . ' She pointed to a rug on the settee. 'Think of the four hundred you're getting.'

'You'll bring it with you?'

Freda nodded gravely. 'But *not until I see his dead body can you have it*.'

'Fair enough.'

They regarded at each other for a second or two. Then:

'Having got it, you go . . . ' Freda pointed to the garden window. ' . . . through the garden, leaving *this window* and the *back gate* open. Your exit ends our relationship.'

Vic frowned, looking uncertain.

'I shall plant the Coca-Cola and glass,' Freda hurried on, 'then run to the porter and raise the alarm. I shall tell the police the money is missing, and that I suspect the boys from the camp. They will go there and question them, and look for the money. They will get nowhere, and it'll all fizzle out in a week.'

She paused, becoming irritated as the man contained to frown, then shake his head.

'Mrs. Nutting,' he said, 'I'm sorry to discourage you, but . . . your murder is *no good*!'

'No good?' Freda was shocked.

'It's easy, all right, like you said. But it's *too* easy . . . too . . . ready-made.'

'Ready-made?'

'Ready-made. So it's not surprising that it doesn't fit.'

'Doesn't fit?'

He began walking about, deep in thought. He turned and looked at her frankly as she stared at him in dismay.

'It's a wonderful murder for a Christmas Club treasurer but it won't do for your *husband*.'

'Why not?'

'Because,' he said patiently, 'your husband is not a Christmas Club treasurer.'

'He's the Bingo treasurer. I don't see . . . ?'

'He is a writer . . . an artist. Therefore he must die like one. Otherwise the coppers will say, 'Hello, hello'!'

'Oh?' Freda was unconvinced. 'And how do writers die?'

'In bed, mostly.'

'Too true they do!' Freda snapped. 'Of old age! I can't wait that long.'

'Despair not, lady! There's a murder here. A convincing, workmanlike murder.' Vic smiled. 'I can feel one coming.'

'You won't think one up in five minutes, I can tell you that.' Freda was unconvinced. 'I've been months on mine.'

She watched him narrowly as he wandered about, deep in thought.

'And don't wander about!' she

27

snapped. 'You're leaving hairs and fibres everywhere! They can put those things under a microscope. They tell your life story.'

He pulled up the hard chair and sat facing her again.

'*My* murder's perfect,' Freda insisted. 'Handed to us on a plate, it is. Money in the house. Those crooks at the camp knowing it's there . . . '

'That's where you've gone wrong,' Vic interrupted. 'You're certain those boys will behave like crooks.'

'How else can they behave?' Freda looked her puzzlement. 'They *are* crooks.'

'*Were* crooks! But down there, free as the air, no bolts or bars, no shouting at them, they're not crooks. They're just happy kids again because of your husband's kindness.'

'Oh, my God!' Freda began to look disconcerted.

'They wouldn't repay that kindness with treachery. More likely . . . show fantastic loyalty.' Vic spread his hands. 'I don't think they'd murder your husband for a million pounds.'

'Don't you?' Freda said, petulantly.

'No. And neither do you. Or you'd have got one of them to do it.'

Freda looked flustered. 'It had to be a stranger . . . unconnected. Look! We'll get nowhere theorising . . . '

'The *police* will theorise,' Vic pointed out.

'Yes,' Freda snapped. 'As follows . . . 'Nutting was a fool trusting those baa-lambs. Money lying about. Asking for it. Well, he's got it.' It won't be '*Was* it them?' but '*Which* of the little bastards was it?''

'Which raises a point.' Vic frowned. 'What if they pin it on one of those boys? They're dogs with bad names, don't forget. He might get life imprisonment.'

'Nonsense!' Freda was dismissive.

'But what if he did! *We* wouldn't be coming forward, would we?'

Freda shrugged. 'They'll probably spend half their lives in prison, anyhow.'

'Maybe. But let it be their doing, not ours.'

There was a long pause, then: 'Are

you going to do this or not?' Freda demanded.

Vic remained deep in thought for a moment, his expression deeply worried. Then his face cleared: he began to get a little excited.

'I've got it! The very murder we want. And we'll get away with it, too. It's not a murder for money at all. It's to do with . . . ' He got up quickly and went over to Howard's bedroom. 'May I see in here again?'

'Yes, all right.'

He opened the door and stood looking in. 'Very self-contained, isn't it?' he remarked.

'He entertains his writing friends in there . . . thank God!' Freda said venomously.

'Do those boys come here at all?'

Freda considered. 'They might come for a railway ticket. Or to take something down.'

'Does he spend much time at the camp?'

'No.'

'No, but you could say that he does.'

His eyes gleamed. 'No female friends, you say? You don't live as man and wife . . . '

'What *is* all this?' Freda was becoming increasingly impatient.

Vic began to laugh, and Freda gave a little start of fear. 'Here, what's the matter with you? You're not a bloody looney, are you?'

He laughed even louder.

'Call yourself clever! And all you could think up in months was a crude burglary job. And all the time, right on your doorstep, was . . . the perfect, professional murder! Made to measure!'

Freda was angry. 'Do you mind if I hear it?'

'Not at all. I'll say straight away, though, mine uses the boys, same as yours. But mine is much more convincing.'

'All right — convince me!' Freda snapped.

'It will be a pleasure.' He came away from surveying the bedroom, looking very pleased with himself.

'Mrs. Nutting, if you line up ten young men and say to them, 'You desperately

31

desire money. Step forward those of you who would murder his friend for a hundred pounds,' you would get no volunteers.'

Turning, he picked up the metal figure. 'But,' he continued, 'if you said, 'Step forward those who would' . . . er . . . ' He swung the metal figure significantly. ' . . . 'defend himself . . . instantly . . . with the first thing to hand . . . against an elderly male seducer . . . ' Then I am quite certain that all ten would step forward as one man. An emotional decision, of course, but one which is in our favour.'

He carefully replaced the metal figure, and turned back to Freda, who was looking at him intently.

'It is this simple fact that we shall take advantage of,' he explained. 'Your husband's slayer will be a young man whom he got in here and to whom he made an . . . outrageous suggestion!'

'Now you're just being stupid!' Freda was indignant. 'Whatever my husband is, he's not *that*!'

'He doesn't have to *be* that,' Vic said

patiently. 'All we require is that the police should *think* he is. Or, rather, *was*. And they're bound to, because you will *say* that he was. And we shall plant evidence to support this.'

'You don't seem so worried about your precious boys *now*,' Freda remarked.

Vic shrugged. 'Nothing to worry *about*.'

'The police'll go to that camp just as fast.'

'Sure, they will,' Vic said. 'Looking for the owner of the fingerprints on the Coca-Cola glass. But they won't find him, will they? So they'll conclude the murderer was a pick-up, a total stranger . . . and they won't expect to see him again . . . or the Bingo money either.'

He paused to study the effect his words were having on her. Then added, 'The whole thing will finish . . . with his funeral. You agree?'

'Your plan is clever,' Freda admitted. 'But we can't use it.'

He raised an eyebrow. 'Can't use it?'

'Not at this late stage,' Freda told him firmly. 'I want the thing done tomorrow.

33

No time to alter things now.'

Vic gave a sigh. 'Look, we alter nothing except your dialogue to the police. You're an actress, aren't you?'

'Yes,' Freda admitted.

'And you can tell a convincing story?'

'Yes.'

'All right — here's your big chance. You'll sit here . . . a bewildered, weeping widow . . . wear your black . . . while the police tenderly, but totally, drag out of you, piece by festering piece, the whole stinking story . . . the misery of your marriage, which was nothing but a social fa¢låde, a cover, for his Jekyll and Hyde sex lark . . . the humiliation of being unwanted, while he — ' He pointed to Howard's bedroom. ' — behind locked doors . . . '

'That door *doesn't* lock,' Freda pointed out.

He turned to examine the door. 'It's got a bolt. Same thing.' He came back to her.

'Tell your story well, Mrs. Nutting, remembering that nobody can contradict any part of it. Least of all, the person most concerned.' He pointed to Howard's picture. 'And the whole country will delight in the dirt, and congratulate you on being rid of him.'

Freda was still undecided.

'You can't go wrong,' he urged. 'You know you can't ... And you've got twenty-four hours to get your story off.' He paused, then: 'Well, what's it to be? S.B. or O.S.?'

She looked at him in puzzlement.

'Surprised Burglar, or Outrageous Suggestion?' he explained. 'O.S. every time, eh? Agree?'

Freda nodded, won over.

'Course you do.' Vic smiled. 'You know we'll get away with it.'

'All right. You win.'

'We *both* win. Because we can't lose. Right. First thing ... we plant some evidence.'

'I think *I* can help there,' Freda said quickly. Crossing to a little-used part of the bookcase, she got out a rather worn envelope containing some postcard-sized photographs. With an odd smile, she handed them to Vic.

Wonderingly, he opened the envelope and looked at them.

'Pornographic studies,' she told him unnecessarily. 'Found here after a party . . . years ago.'

'I'll believe you.' He smiled faintly. 'Thousands wouldn't.' He continued to look at the photographs.

'Haven't dated, have they?' Freda commented, dryly.

'No.'

'After the party, nobody claimed them, naturally.'

'They get the police out when they lose a Rembrandt,' Vic grunted.

Freda obtained a duster and began wiping the pictures, back and front. 'Make sure my fingerprints are not on them.'

When she had finished wiping them, he took the photographs from her, and put them back in the envelope.

'Just the job,' he said in satisfaction. 'Now, we need one or two bits of . . . er . . . underwear, and a spot of make-up.'

Freda headed to her bedroom, and after a moment's thought, Vic returned to

Howard's bedroom.

At length, Freda came back with the items he had requested: panties, bra, and make-up.

She looked around, wondering where he had gone. Seconds later, he came out of the bedroom. She showed him the articles. 'These do?'

'Lovely,' he approved. He pointed into Howard's bedroom. 'That bottom drawer of his. It's got a key. Is he likely to go there for anything?'

'No. Only old underwear there, for throwing out.'

'Right,' he decided. 'I'll lock all this in there.'

He took the items into the bedroom and came back with the key. 'That drawer is his guilty hidey-hole,' he elaborated. He held up the key. 'You put this on his body, on his key-ring. O.K.?'

'O.K.,' she assented, and held out her hand for the key.

'The police will ask what key it is, and that sparks off your tragic story,' he told her. 'Put it away safe till you want it.'

He watched as she put it in the

sideboard drawer. 'Right. Now, how about a quick run-through?'

'O.K. Go.'

Vic became animated. 'You leave here tomorrow evening, six-thirty, after unbolting side door. On way out you get porter to buzz husband . . . have you left gas on? Proves he's alive. Off you go to your club, where you meet Lucy for drinks. You sit near the telephone box . . . '

'Correct.' Freda nodded.

'I arrive, side door, soon after. I let myself in . . . '

'Bolting the door after you,' Freda said quickly.

'Don't tell me. I want to be sure I know. I have a torch. I find my way up the stone stairs to this door.'

'How are you dressed?' Freda asked.

'To pass for Telephone Engineer. Overalls and shoes, disposable, spare shoes in tool-bag. Also paper carrier bag . . . Ah-ah!' He broke off with a sudden realization, and frowned.

'What is it?'

'Telephone Engineer's no good — they

don't come out at night, except if it's an emergency. A noisy line's not an emergency.'

He looked around the room quickly, and his gaze took in the television set. 'That telly . . . is it rented?'

'Yes.'

Vic blew out his cheeks. 'Our luck's in. Who's the rental firm?'

' 'Tops T.V.' '

'Couldn't be better.' Vic smiled. 'I'm the Tops T.V. man. Tomorrow,' he went on, pointing to the telephone, 'call Tops and request them to send someone to service your set. Do it at four o'clock.'

Freda frowned. 'But what if the genuine man comes?'

'What, the same evening?' He shook his head. 'You'll be lucky. Right, I'm the T.V. man. I ring the bell. He answers. Er . . . could we . . . act this out, Mrs. Nutting? I'd like to get the feel of it.' Turning, he picked up the cushion. 'It's pretty quick once he opens the door.'

'Of course. Let me look first.' Freda opened the door and looked out. 'O.K., the coast's clear.'

He went out, and she closed the door. Seconds later the bell rang, and she opened the door. Vic was standing there, the cushion — representing the tool-bag — in his left hand.

'Tops T.V., sir. You requested a service.'

'No, no,' Freda said sharply. 'Ask his name first.'

'Of course. Sorry!' Vic went out again and shut the door.

The bell rang again, and she opened the door. He was standing there as before.

'Mr. Nutting?' he inquired.

'That's right.'

'Tops T.V., sir. You requested a service?'

Freda nodded. 'Come in,' she invited.

Vic took three paces into the room. Then, while she was closing the door, he put down his 'bag' as though about to take off his gloves.

As he was straightening up, she crossed in front of him to the T.V. With a smooth continuation of his straightening move-ment, Vic grabbed the metal figure and made a pantomime of striking her from behind.

She turned to him. 'All right? Nothing wrong with *that*!'

'Perfect,' he agreed, carefully replacing the metal figure.

'You'll leave that on the floor, naturally,' Freda said as she replaced the cushion.

'Naturally,' Vic assented.

'Right.' Freda gave him a keen look. 'What next?'

'I throw the rug over him. I pick up phone, send signal.'

'No,' Freda said sharply. 'You'll need to get rid of your shoes and overalls first.'

'O.K. I take off shoes and overalls. I wrap shoes in overalls, put in paper carrier. I put on spare shoes. *Then* I pick up phone and send signal.'

He moved to the telephone, consulting his cigarette packet on the way. As he picked up the receiver to dial, Freda waved her hand negatively.

'Close the line first.'

He looked puzzled.

Freda walked forward to the phone and held the studs down. 'Not tomorrow.

Now. The exchange might hear us.'

He attempted to dial, but found he was unable to do so. 'Can't dial with my gloves on,' he said.

Freda had the answer. 'Use the pencil. It's over there on the desk.'

He picked up the pencil and dialled, then: 'When you pick up to answer, I tap . . . ' He tapped the mouthpiece. ' . . . twice, once, twice again. We both hang up.' He did so, replacing the pencil. 'That O.K.?'

'O.K.'

'Right. Now, where will the Bingo money be?'

Freda pointed. 'On the desk. Or in this drawer. You take it and you wait for me. That's all. I'll be here at nine.' She looked at him coldly, then added: 'When you show me his dead body, I give you the four hundred.'

When he didn't say anything, Freda raised her eyebrows. Catching her look, Vic spoke deliberately. 'You need to understand one thing, Mrs. Nutting.'

'What's that?'

'I'm completely trusting you. You must

completely trust me. If not . . . somebody might get hurt.'

Freda frowned. 'What do you mean by that?'

'I mean, when you come with the money, don't bring your boyfriend.'

Freda tensed, looking at him in surprise.

'Don't tell me there isn't one,' Vic said dryly.

Freda relaxed, shrugging. 'There certainly is,' she admitted. 'And he is very dear to me. That's why none of this will touch him. He'll be miles away. And he'll know nothing but what the papers tell him . . . ever.' She looked at him challengingly.

'Fair enough.' He smiled faintly. 'Please excuse my mentioning it.'

'Of course.'

'Right. You return, the financial side is completed, and I go, taking my bag, and leaving — ' He pointed to the garden window. ' — through that window and the back gate open.'

'Making sure nobody sees you,' Freda said quickly.

'Naturally. Right. You're on your own. What do you do then?'

'I work fast because the porter saw me come in . . . ' Freda hesitated. 'This is the bit that's been altered.'

'Now, don't panic. You've three things to remember . . . pictures, Coca-Cola, key.'

'Pictures, I strew on the floor. Coca-Cola, I open, put some in the glass. Key . . . ' Freda hesitated again.

'That's most important.'

'I put on his key-ring.'

He nodded. 'Then . . . you start screaming.'

'Yes.'

'Mention the boy early . . . to the police,' Vic advised. 'As soon as your husband got in, he asked if somebody called Terry had phoned.' He pointed to the sideboard cupboard. 'It's Terry's fingerprints on the glass. Terry's the lad who did it. Get that clear in your mind.'

'Yes.'

'Don't be anxious to give information. Let the police drag it out of you. Tell them everything, but reluctantly, with disgust . . . ' Breaking off, he went into Howard's bedroom, then continued, ' . . . how he entertained boys in here . . . with the door bolted.' He tried the bolt, then looked at Freda sharply. 'This bolt is stiff — it won't move. Good job I looked. Wants a drop of oil.'

'Oil?' Freda asked, blankly.

'Hair oil, anything.'

'There'll be something in the bathroom,' Freda responded, turning.

Vic had stooped, looking through the keyhole of Howard's door. 'And a bit of cotton wool,' he called.

Freda nodded and continued her journey to the bathroom. Almost immediately she came back with hair oil and cotton wool.

She gave him the hair oil and watched as he oiled the bolt. Finishing the small task, he returned the hair oil to her and took the cotton wool.

'What's the cotton wool for?'

He stuffed some in the keyhole, and explained. 'He said there was a draught. It was so you couldn't see in.' He returned the surplus cotton wool to her.

'Tiny details . . . but very important.'

Freda returned the items to the bathroom, coming back at once. She saw that he was making sure that the bolt was now working all right.

He glanced up at her.

'Get your story down pat. All the different parts. The mockery of your marriage. Your loneliness. Your inability to act or complain . . . ' His gaze shifted to take in Howard's picture again, swung back to his wife. ' . . . being dependent on him. His brother, the one that was drowned. Use him, too.'

Freda wrinkled her brow. 'How can I do that?'

Vic spread his hands. 'He warned your husband . . . repeatedly . . . to keep away from the camp. Convincing stuff, that. Remember the great golden truth: the bigger the lie, the more they believe it.' He took a closer look at the picture. 'Is that a cut over his eye?'

'Yes, a car accident.'

'No.' Vic pointed to Howard's bedroom. 'He got that in there . . . from a beer bottle.' He replaced the picture.

'You've got twenty-four hours. Time to think up all sorts of convincing little details. Make your story exciting . . . ' He added, dryly: 'Remember, I shall be reading it.'

Freda nodded eagerly. 'Now I've got used to the idea, I can see it's a thousand times better.'

'And you're getting it for the same price. Anything you're still worried about?'

'Not a thing.'

'Right. Then that only leaves . . . ' He made a gesture of financial anticipation with his fingertips.

Freda pointed to the desk drawer. 'One hundred pounds. In that drawer.'

Opening the drawer, he found the money. After looking at it briefly, he slipped it into his pocket.

'The rest . . . ' Freda paused. ' . . . the four hundred . . . '

'Over his dead body,' Vic finished for her. 'Mrs. Nutting, it's a pleasure to do business with you!'

Freda held out a hand. 'Give me your gloves.'

He did so, and she put them in the drawer in the sideboard. 'I'll show you out the side door, the way you come in tomorrow. You can see the lie of the land.'

They headed towards the door together. Before opening it, Freda looked at him for a second. 'Good luck tomorrow, Vic.'

He smiled. 'Thank you, Mrs. Nutting, and the same to you.'

She opened the door carefully, making sure that nobody was about before they went out, leaving the door ajar.

Behind them the phone rang briefly, then stopped.

On her return, Freda shut the door, and stood for a while, deep in thought. Then she went over to the buzzer and dialled.

'Porter . . . ? Ernie, darling, it's Mrs. Nutting . . . the furnished flat upstairs, which came empty. I spoke to you about it for a business acquaintance of mine, a Mr. Bliss, and he promised you a definite 'yes' or 'no' today. Well, I've been trying to get him all day at his office, and . . . What . . . ? He phoned you . . . ? He's taken it? He's in . . . ?' She looked up at the ceiling. 'He's there now . . . ? Well, he's a fast worker!'

Her face was wreathed in smiles. The porter's news had made her very happy.

'Thank you for telling me . . . What? The deposit . . . ? The agreement . . . ? Don't worry! He's a bit absent-minded, dear. I'll get on to him straight away . . . What's his number . . . ? Thank you, Ernie . . . Be seeing you . . . Bye.'

She hung up, then went to the telephone and dialled.

She was kept waiting for a reply. Puzzled, she glanced at the ceiling a few times. She lit a cigarette, continuing to listen. At length, she got a response. Quickly, she answered with a secure and happy intimacy, making kissing noises. 'Guess who . . . ? Bernard! You sly puss! You're in! Ernie's just told me . . . I've been trying to get you all day . . . You called me just now . . . ? Ah, I *thought* I heard it ring . . . '

Her voice suddenly became grave and secret.

'Darling, I've got the most wonderful

news, so come down straight away and hear it . . . Me come up? Why can't you come down . . . ? You're just going to have a bath . . . You're starkers . . . ? Then I don't think I better had come up!'

She let out a peal of wicked laughter.

'Yes . . . Yes, my pet . . . ?' Freda's bantering tone became serious. 'You seem so down, my darling . . . Of course it's that bloody wife of yours. You don't have to *tell* me . . . She called you at your *office*? She said *that* over the telephone . . . ? Well, of course it'll be all over the building tomorrow . . . '

Freda continued to listen to the voice on the other end of her line for a while, then came to a decision.

'Bernard, I won't have you treated like this,' she said firmly. 'We're going to stop Madam Janet's gallop once and for all. Are you listening . . . ? Have you got pen and paper handy? And an envelope . . . ?'

Freda waited a moment, then:

' . . . Bernard? Now, you just write exactly what I say . . . ready? 'Damn you. Stop pestering me. Thanks for the memory. Goodbye. Bernard.' Address the

envelope . . . hat is going in the post tonight, and I'll see that it does . . . *I've* got a stamp. And don't seal it. I want to be sure you've written what I said. Just let her have *that* with her cornflakes . . . '
She paused.

'Feeling better now . . . ?' Freda looked up at the ceiling. 'Do you know what I keep on doing? I keep on looking at the ceiling and thinking to myself . . . My man . . . my wonderful *man* . . . is just the other side of that plaster! Bump the floor, dear . . . Bump the floor . . . I want to see if the chandelier shakes . . . What . . . ?'

She released a peal of sexy laughter.

'You are shocking, really . . . You've got something round you, haven't you . . . ? Not getting cold . . . ? But I must let you go, otherwise we shall be late for the theatre . . . '

She picked up an envelope containing a theatre ticket.

'Which reminds me, dear, why did you send *my* ticket through the post . . . ? You're going to be late . . . ? You *were* going to be late . . . ? And now the appointment's cancelled? Well, thank God for that . . . I'll hang up, then. You get your bath . . . What? *My* news . . . ? *Just you wait till you hear . . .*

'No, dear, not over the phone . . . Well, just a hint, then, just to take your mind off that God-awful wife of yours . . . Are you listening . . . ? All ready for a lovely surprise . . . ?'

Her voice became edged and low.

'You know the job we've wanted done for so long . . . ? The five hundred job . . . ? I've found a young man who'll do it . . . So just you hurry down and hear all about it . . . And, darling . . . Don't forget your name is Bliss . . . '

She made more kissing noises before hanging up.

2

It was six-fifteen the following evening. In the Nutting household, the curtains were drawn and the lights on. Both the bedroom doors and the kitchen door were open.

Author Howard Nutting was at his desk, reading the pages of his latest typescript. From time to time, he screwed up some of the pages and threw them into the paper bin.

He was quite evidently becoming distracted by the sounds of Freda's singing to herself in the bathroom. Above the singing sounds came that of a lavatory flush being operated. After a moment, Freda emerged from the bathroom and went into her bedroom. She was watchful of Howard as she crossed the room.

Freda was clearly preparing to go out, and from time to time she emerged from the bedroom to check her appearance in the living-room mirror.

Her breathy, self-conscious singing and inability to relax were indicative of her sense of guilt, and not a little fear.

Howard was showing increasing irritation as her vocal efforts continued to interrupt his concentration. For her own part, while pretending to ignore her husband, Freda was very carefully noting everything he was doing.

At length she switched on a transistor radio, releasing an avalanche of pent-up pop.

Howard lost his patience. He turned in his chair, and glared towards Freda's bedroom. 'For God's sake! Freda!'

Freda appeared in her bedroom doorway.

'Yes, Howard?'

'Must you?'

'Must I what, dear?'

Howard pointed to the offending radio. 'Must you have that bloody row blaring out?' He was almost shouting with frustration. 'I'm trying to think!'

'Oh! Sorry, darling!' Freda touched the transistor and quiet was restored. 'I thought you liked a little music some-times.'

Howard returned to looking at his script again. 'I like a *little* music *anytime*,' he said heavily.

After glancing at the clock, Freda crossed over to the desk, picked up the paper bin and made her way to the door with it. She halted as Howard spoke sharply.

'And where are you going with that?'

Freda affected surprise. 'To empty it, dear.'

'Why?'

'Because it's full.'

Howard's annoyance was obvious by his tone. '*Not* 'why empty it'. I *know* why paper bins are emptied. *Why* empty it *now*?'

Freda shrugged. 'I'm afraid the answer is the same. Because it's full.'

'It's barely half-full!'

'I should hate to argue, but . . . ' Freda tilted the bin to show him its contents.

'That'll push down!' Howard snapped testily. 'And why empty it at *this* time of night? Especially when I'm *using* it?'

'I like the place tidy,' Freda said mildly.

Howard snorted. 'Since when, for God's sake? House pride, Freda, is something you will never suffer from.'

'One doesn't suffer from it,' Freda demurred. 'One aspires to it.'

'Well, don't aspire to it just now!' Howard snapped. He got up and grabbed the bin from her, slamming it down on the floor and back into service. Then he turned back to the sorting of his papers. 'If ever I come home, Freda, and find this place tidy, I'll drop dead in the doorway.'

Freda frowned. 'I just don't believe that.' For a few moments she stood, baffled. Then she picked up her handbag and began rummaging in it.

'Oh! Now I've no cigarettes! I'll have to buy some more.' She took out some money and started for the door. 'I'll pop out and see my friend Ernie.'

'Here you are.' Howard slapped his own packet of cigarettes on the end of the desk nearest to her.

Freda pretended not to have heard, and opened the door.

'I said, 'Here you are'.' Howard's voice

rose in exasperation.

Freda stopped, and turned. 'You *know* I don't like your brand, dear.'

'Since when?'

'I never smoke *those* now, Howard. They're just coffin nails, nothing but.'

Howard looked at her in amazement, then shrugged and took his cigarettes back again.

'Best news I've heard for some time,' he grunted.

'You say the sweetest things,' Freda said sarcastically and swept out of the room, leaving the door open.

Howard turned back to looking at his typescript. He decided to finish with it for the moment, and carefully laid it aside. Taking up the cloth money bag he untied it, emptying the contents on to the desk. He started to count it, jotting his findings on a slip of paper as he did so.

At length Freda returned with cigarettes she had purchased from the porter, and went on with her preparations for departure: seeing to her face in the mirror, trying on her hat. She saw that her husband was now counting the money.

Whilst looking into the mirror, she commented: 'If there's any over, I know a very deserving cause.'

Her husband ignored her remark.

'The Freda Nutting Foundation,' she added dryly.

Howard tightened his lips. 'Are you hinting you're short of money?'

'Not hinting. Stating.'

'I'm afraid you can't have any of this. You'll have to wait till tomorrow.'

Freda turned and regarded him. 'I've enough for tonight.'

Howard appeared to notice for the first time that his wife was preparing to go out.

'You going out?'

'It's Monday night,' Freda answered dismissively, putting on her lipstick. Her tone suggested she was addressing a backward child.

Howard was needled. 'I know damn well it's Monday night,' he snapped.

'Then if you know 'damn well' it's Monday night,' Freda retorted, addressing him through the mirror, 'you should know 'damn well' what I do . . . and where I go . . . on Monday nights, shouldn't you?'

Howard's anger increased, the penny not yet having dropped.

'It's my Lucy night,' Freda added.

'Lucy . . . ?'

Freda turned in feigned exasperation. 'Oh, my God! Lucy Lamont, 1956 tour of *Make Him Say 'Please'*. We meet at her Club for gin and memories . . . every Monday . . . remember?'

Howard frowned. 'It was *Tuesday* for years.'

'Was it, dear?' Freda pretended surprise. 'Well, we changed it.'

'Then why the hell don't you say so?'

'I thought I was, dear.' Freda suddenly remembered something with high-pitched alarm. 'Oh!'

Howard gave a start. 'Must you?'

'I just remembered something I had to tell you. Vitally important! Telly's gone wonky.'

'Huh!' Her husband gave a snort of derision. 'The telly's the *least* of my worries!'

'But not the least of mine. I'm coming back to see something . . . at 9.05.'

'Then you'll be unlucky, won't you?'

'No.' Freda smiled. 'I phoned for service.'

'When?'

'This afternoon.'

Howard laughed. 'And you expect them tonight? Where did you say we lived? Buckingham Palace?'

Freda was unfazed. 'Well, if he *does* come . . . '

Howard had finished counting the money. Suddenly fancying a drink, he rose from his seat. He looked at his wife as he crossed to the sideboard. 'If he happens to come just as I'm leaving, I shall tell him to go to hell.'

He fixed himself a drink as his wife put the finishing touches to herself at the mirror.

'Good idea. He might make you . . . ' Freda gave a quiet chuckle. ' . . . late.'

Howard picked up his drink thoughtfully.

'While you're over there, dear, bring me my coat, will you?' Freda asked.

Howard put down his drink on the sideboard and crossed to where the coats were. 'What are you wearing?' he asked.

'Tonight, dear?' Freda paused and smiled faintly. 'Tonight I'll wear my black.'

He brought the black coat over to her, holding it out for her to slip into. Then he picked up his drink and returned to his desk again. He reached for the pages of typescript.

Now ready to depart, Freda paused and turned to him again. She looked at him for a few seconds.

'Did you start your new play at the camp as you intended?'

'I did.'

'What's it about?'

Howard frowned, expelled a breath in a deep sigh. 'Freda, you can't ask that question with your hat and coat on and your hand on the doorknob.'

'My hand isn't on the doorknob, dear.'

Howard waved a hand dismissively. 'I'll tell you tomorrow.'

She crossed to him and gave him a little routine peck. 'Clever boy,' she murmured.

Howard was moved to make some sort of brief comment about his new play. 'It won't appeal to you. You like everybody to live happy ever after.'

'Not *everybody*, dear.' She moved to the door and opened it. 'That would be stupid. Bye, dear.'

The door closed behind her.

Howard sat for a moment, looking at his papers. Then he decided to leave what he had been doing; he needed to get dressed himself before he went out. He had only just got into his bedroom when the buzzer sounded.

He came out of his bedroom and took the call. 'Yes . . . ? Yes, Ernie, put her on . . . Yes, what is it, Freda? The gas . . . ? Hang on . . . '

Putting down the mouthpiece, he went into kitchen to check the cooker, returning almost at once and taking up the mouthpiece again.

'The cooker's not on, Freda, how could it be? We didn't cook anything . . . Coffee . . . ? Well, there's nothing on . . . No smell, either . . . Bye . . . '

Hanging up, he returned to his

bedroom and put on a record. After a moment some soothing nice music was heard. A little later he came out in his shirtsleeves, and went into the bathroom.

The sound of the music was spoiled by the ringing of the doorbell. Howard came out of the bathroom using a small hand towel, and went into his bedroom.

The music stopped. He came out of his bedroom without the hand towel as the doorbell rang again.

'All right! All right! Don't be so bloody impatient!' He crossed and opened the door.

A woman he had never seen before was standing outside. She was about thirty, perhaps a little younger, and smartly dressed. She carried a handbag and was wearing gloves. As he stared at her in surprise, he saw that she was taut, apprehensive — she appeared to be keyed up with some strong fear.

Her emotional state was such that Howard was momentarily taken aback.

'Good evening,' the woman faltered. 'I . . . er . . . '

'Good evening,' Howard responded cautiously.

'Does a . . . a Mrs. Nutting live here?' the woman resumed hesitantly. 'Mrs. *Howard* Nutting?'

'She does. Do you want her?'

'Yes, I . . . '

'Then I'm afraid you're unlucky,' Howard said gently. 'She's just gone out.'

'Oh — '

'You've only just missed her; she only left a few seconds ago . . . ' He frowned at a sudden thought. 'You're not Tops T.V., are you?'

'Not what?' The woman looked at him blankly.

'No, of course not.' Howard smiled apologetically. 'Damn silly thing to say. But, you know, these days . . . shortage of men . . . ' He paused and looked at her again, sensing something wrong. 'Was it important . . . what you wanted to see her about?'

The woman bit her lip.

'I'm *Mr.* Nutting. Can I help?' He smiled, then his expression changed to one of concern as the woman suddenly gave way to uncontrolled weeping.

'Good God! Are you all right?' He grabbed hold of her shoulders. 'You're ill or something.'

Her weeping grew worse, having found a shoulder.

'Look! Hadn't you better come in?' Howard helped her in, closing the door quickly.

'That's it. Come in and sit down for a moment.' He led her towards the settee, and helped her as she slumped into it.

'Here we are . . . Now, we'll see what is going on . . . sort it out if we can. You just sit there for a bit, and I'll get you a drop of something.'

Howard was on his way to the sideboard when he suddenly stopped as a thought struck him. 'You're not in any pain, are you?'

The woman was now recovered a little. She seemed surprised at Howard's question.

'Pain?'

'I mean . . . alcohol might be all wrong . . . perhaps I should call a doctor.'

'I don't need a doctor. I'm not in any

pain.' As she saw him hesitating, she added: 'I don't need any alcohol, either.'

He came back and stood looking at her.

'I'm sorry,' she said. 'It's been . . . boiling up.'

'And now it's . . . boiled over.' She smiled a little, as she recovered herself. 'What's been boiling up?'

'It's nothing.' She sniffed. 'Nothing at all . . . '

'"Nothing at all" doesn't boil over,' Howard said firmly. 'Neither does it produce drama such as this. I happen to be a writer — a dramatist — and I know.'

The woman sniffed again, and looked up. 'It's something I have to see your wife about. I'll . . . come back when she's here.' She made to rise from the settee. 'I'll go now.'

Howard stepped forward and pushed her gently but firmly back to where she was.

'You will *not* go now,' he said kindly. She stared at him, wide-eyed. 'You can't walk into my house, er . . . boil over, and then walk out, without even saying who you are, or why you came. You say it concerns my wife. Then, as my wife's husband, I probably have a legal right to know.' He looked at her expectantly, but she shook her head.

'It would be better if I went.'

'Not for me,' Howard insisted. 'I should be a nervous wreck before bedtime, wondering why you came.' As the woman remained silent, Howard frowned. 'This isn't a little hobby of yours, is it? Knocking on people's doors, getting a lot of attention, and then . . . ?'

'Of course not!' Her voice was sharp with indignation.

'Sorry,' Howard apologised. 'But you know how it is these days. People . . . identity-starved . . . '

'Don't include me. I've a little too much of it at the moment.'

'Sorry.' Howard paused, then tried again: 'Well, when you're ready, we'll start. First of all, who are you?'

'I'm Mrs. Bernard Webb. I live near here. I've been married . . . seven years.' Her voice faltered again. 'They've been . . . seven happy years . . . '

'Mrs. Bernard Webb, I believe you. I

congratulate you — indeed, I envy you — but what's it got to do with my wife?

'Don't you know?' She looked surprised.

'Should I ask, if I did?'

'Your wife's breaking up my home . . . ' she said briefly, hardening her voice.

Howard looked at her in shock and dismay. '*What?*'

'Stealing my husband, that's what your wife is doing.'

There was an awkward pause.

Howard shook his head at the accusation. 'I think you've come to the wrong address.'

The woman was not to be diverted. 'Mrs. Howard Nutting, Flat Five, Kingston Court, South West One — there aren't *two*, surely?'

'Then you've made some horrible mistake . . . '

'Mr. Nutting! That kind of mistake is not made.'

Howard was visibly shaken by the woman's obvious sincerity. 'I . . . I can't think what to say. I'm so shocked.'

'What about me? I've prayed for weeks

that it's some sort of joke . . . that some awful man with a microphone will pop up and say, 'It's all a giggle, dear. Have a washing machine.''

She looked at him closely. 'And you genuinely didn't know . . . anything?

'I told you.' Howard was thinking swiftly. 'But . . . that's not really surprising.'

'Why?' It was her turn to look surprised.

'Never mind . . . ' Howard paused, then: 'How long has this been going on?'

'Goodness knows. We're the last to know, you may depend on that.' She looked at him searchingly. 'Are you very much in love with your wife?'

'I'm not in love with her at all,' Howard admitted frankly.

'So that's what you meant?'

'Meant?' Howard wrinkled his brow.

'You said you didn't know, and 'but that's not really surprising'. If you'll excuse my saying so, you *wouldn't* know, would you . . . I mean, if you didn't care.'

'I care about you being hurt,' Howard said quietly.

'I'm sorry.'

'Don't be . . . ' Howard paused, reflecting. 'I'm not quite certain what happened to our marriage. Started the same as others . . . God knows where it went then. Just weren't suited, I suppose.'

'You've no children?'

Howard shook his head. 'No. Maybe that's why we've no marriage. They say children can save a marriage.'

'I know.' Their eyes met. 'It's a theory we can't test, either.'

'My plays are my babies; my writing, my mistress, I suppose,' Howard mused. 'Writing is a kind of loving, I imagine. You've got to give everything . . . otherwise it doesn't work . . . nothing comes back. Perhaps I can't do both . . . ' He paused, smiled bitterly. 'My wife has her job, her friends. When we meet, we try not to be rude to each other.'

'She has a job?'

Howard nodded. 'Bits in television, modelling sometimes, but . . . '

'But what?'

'*Had* a job would be nearer the truth.

The kids get all the work now.' He smiled. 'Thank God they can't write.'

'How old is she?'

'Thirty. What about Bernard?'

'Twenty-eight. He's in a travel agency . . . ' She paused. 'Mr. Nutting, has your wife any . . . influence . . . in television?'

'Influence?'

'My husband took part in a documentary at his place of business. Ever since, he's been ambitious to become an actor in television.'

'Thousands of would-be actors end up on the dole.'

'Yes, but there are shortcuts, I suppose. If she said she had influence . . . You see, I'm hoping it's something like that, and not . . . the real thing.'

Howard reflected, then nodded. 'You may be right. That may be what's going on.' He began to wander about restlessly. 'I'm not *involved* like you are. Makes me feel awful. I'm not even humiliated. Just angry.'

'I understand.'

Howard stopped pacing and swung

about. 'She won't get away with this! By God, she won't . . . Have you talked to your husband about this?'

'I talked him out of the house. He went to sleep at his club. The club porter says he's still there. But I don't think so.'

'Why do you think that?'

'Yesterday, while I was out, he came and took quite a bit of luggage.'

'Did you think he'd come here?'

'I only knew it was a Mrs. Nutting. She might have been a widow. I found out her telephone number, and from that I got her address.'

'When did he go to sleep at his club?' Howard asked, thinking.

'Ten nights ago.'

Howard smiled without mirth. 'I've been away for two weeks. I got back today.'

'He's got that club porter well-trained, I will say that for him . . . ' She paused. 'When I found he'd collected luggage, I called him at his office, a thing he'd told me never to do — the switchboard girls listen for domestic tit-bits — but I was very angry. I said things I shouldn't have.

He hung up on me.'

Mrs. Webb took from her bag a letter without an envelope and gave it to him. 'This morning, I got this.'

He read the letter in silence, then the last bit aloud: ' "Thanks for the memory." How horribly cruel.'

His sympathy was suddenly too much for her. She started to weep again. Instinctively, he sought to console her.

'Now, now ... don't upset yourself again.'

'I'm sorry.' She sniffed miserably.

'Look here! Tomorrow ... we'll ... '

'Tomorrow?' She looked puzzled.

'I've ... an important dinner tonight.'

'And I'm delaying you. You'll have to finish dressing for it.'

'No mad rush!'

She rose from the settee and delved into her bag. 'If I could just tidy up ... then I'll go.'

'Take your time. Take your time ... I'm not expecting anyone ... '

As if in lie to his words, the doorbell rang.

They looked at each other.

'It's her.' Mrs. Webb sounded frightened.

'Can't be.' Howard shook his head emphatically. 'She's got her key.'

'Then who is it?'

'No idea. Soon see.' On his way to the door, Howard suddenly stopped, remembering. 'Oh! It'll be the T.V. repair man. She phoned for service. Coming back at nine to see something.' He started for the door again. 'To hell with her. I'll get rid of him.'

'No!' she exclaimed. As he looked at her over his shoulder, she added: 'Not if she's coming back to see something.'

Howard paused, deliberating; then: 'As you wish.'

The doorbell rang again and Howard moved to open the door. As he was about to open it, Mrs. Webb said plaintively: 'He'll see I've been crying.' She looked at him beseechingly.

Howard pointed to the open door of his bedroom. 'O.K. You'd better hop in there.'

Taking her belongings, she hurried into

his bedroom, leaving the door slightly ajar.

Howard opened the door.

The man who had called himself Vic was standing there, tense and smiling. He was now wearing overalls, canvas shoes, and leather gloves, and held in his left hand an old tool-bag.

The two men stood looking at each other.

'Mr. Nutting?' Vic asked.

'That's right.'

'Tops T.V., sir. Request for service.'

'Come in,' Howard invited.

Vic stepped into the room, taking a quick look about him. While Howard was closing the door, he put down his bag as though to take off his gloves.

As he was straightening, Howard crossed in front of him to the television set.

'Mr. Nutting!' Mrs. Webb's voice sounded from his bedroom. Howard changed direction and headed towards it, pointing to the T.V. as he did so.

'Set's over there. Help yourself.'

Vic stood unmoving for a second,

considerably shaken, and not a little disgusted. He was thinking: 'No women friends! Lying bitch!'

As Howard came out of his bedroom, heading for the kitchen, he saw that Vic had not moved. He pointed to the set again. 'Over there, laddie.'

'Yes, sir.'

Howard went into the kitchen.

Vic picked up his bag and went to the set, where he commenced to pretend that he was servicing it.

Howard came out of the kitchen almost at once with an aspirin and a glass of water.

'Can you tell me what's wrong with this, sir?' Vic asked.

Howard slowed, shrugging. 'You should tell *us*, surely.'

'I mean, sir, what's the complaint?'

'I understand it's wonky.' Howard went into his bedroom and came out almost at once. 'Whatever it is, fix it as soon as you can. I've got to go out.' He moved over to the sideboard and fixed himself a drink. He then went to his desk, taking his drink with him.

Mrs. Webb, having done her repairs to her tearful face, came out of the bedroom, bringing the aspirin and glass with her. She exchanged the barest of glances with Vic, and went over to the settee where Howard met her.

She gave him the aspirin and the glass, and said: 'Thank you. I'm going now.'

Vic glanced at her over his shoulder.

'There's plenty of time yet,' Howard demurred.

'No. You've got to get dressed to go out.'

Howard pointed to the settee. 'Park there for a moment at least, and write down your number for me.' As she complied with his request, Howard put the aspirin bottle and the glass on the table behind the settee. Fetching his directory, he gave it to her, along with a pen. 'Address too.'

While she wrote down her details. Howard joined her on the settee. He looked at what she had written. 'Quite close by,' he commented.

'I told you that.'

Vic, who had been observing them very

closely, now seemed to make up his mind about something. He came forward.

'Excuse me, Mr. Nutting, might I ask a favour?' Howard and the woman gave a start, having forgotten he was there. 'I've been cruising round looking for a phone box, sir.'

Howard gave him a puzzled stare.

'But those I found were out of order, sir.'

As Howard frowned, Mrs. Webb came to his rescue. 'I think he wants to make a call.'

'Why the hell doesn't he say so?' Howard pointed to the phone. 'Over there.'

Vic put a hand in his pocket. 'I've got the sixpence, sir,' he began.

'Forget it. Then get that goggle-box fixed.'

Vic went over to the phone, consulting his cigarette packet on the way. He began to dial with a pencil and waited, stuffing his cigarette packet away in his overalls.

Howard looked concernedly at Mrs. Webb. 'You sure you feel all right? You still look . . . '

'What?'

'Taut . . . as hell. Overwound.'

'That's rather how I feel.'

Howard was holding her hand. 'You've got to try to unwind.'

Across the room, Vic was looking at them over his shoulder. They seemed to have forgotten him again. He noticed, too, the pile of money on the desk. Impulsively, he picked up a bundle of the money and looked at it lovingly. Getting his connection on the phone, he quickly put the money back. Then, pretending a sudden rhythmic mood in tango time, he tapped the mouthpiece twice, once, then twice again. After which, he hung up without speaking.

Mrs. Webb gave a little laugh. 'I'll strain every nerve.' She very gently disengaged her hand, and rose. 'I'll go now.'

Howard rose with her. 'You don't have to . . . because I have to. Stay here a bit and relax.'

'Relax? With Freda heading this way? I'm not the relaxing sort, anyhow.'

'You're the sort that needs a little

alcohol. Eh?' Howard smiled. 'A little one for the road?

'A spot of brandy, then.'

Howard suddenly became aware of Vic as he headed for the sideboard.

'No reply,' Vic told him, nodding to the replaced phone as he made his way back to the T.V. below the settee.

Standing in front to the settee, Mrs. Webb suddenly experienced a dizzy spell, and with a little groan began swaying alarmingly.

Seeing her distress, and being nearer to her than Howard, Vic came smartly to her assistance. He grabbed hold of her, catching her before she could fall. ''Ere lady, what's this? Whoa! Steady there!'

Howard, at the sideboard cupboard, saw what was happening and hurried back, leaving the cupboard door open.

'Went a bit dizzy or something, sir,' Vic told him. 'So I grabbed her. Looked like falling, she did.'

Mrs. Webb managed to speak. 'Yes, I suddenly . . . '

'All right, I've got her now.' Howard took over the situation, and settled Mrs.

Webb on the settee, where she sat looking somewhat lost.

Vic began moving away.

'Here, you!' Howard called him back. 'I don't know your name.'

'Vic, sir.'

'In that sideboard cupboard, Vic!' Howard pointed to it. 'Brandy. Bring some . . . for this lady.'

Vic went quickly over to the sideboard, found the brandy and a glass, and poured some.

Mrs. Webb was recovering. She looked at Howard. 'I do apologise . . . '

'Never mind that . . . '

'Felt awful, suddenly. Quite horrid!'

'Overwound. Didn't I say?'

She smiled wanly. 'I'm just being an awful nuisance tonight.'

Unnoticed, the approaching Vic was listening and watching them intently. There was a strange gleam in his eyes.

'You are not a nuisance.' Howard turned as Vic arrived with the brandy. 'That's a good chap.' Vic retired back to his 'servicing'.

Howard gave the brandy to Mrs. Webb,

who took only the barest sip. 'More than that,' he instructed. She obeyed. 'I just wish I didn't have this dinner tonight,' he muttered.

Their voices dropped to hushed whispers.

'What for?' she asked.

'To get at Freda, that's what for,' Howard growled. 'Apply a little reasoning.'

They gradually began to talk louder, forgetting that Vic was there. For his part, he was listening carefully to every word.

'I have a feeling it's too late for that,' she sighed.

'I'll do more than reason,' Howard vowed. 'I'm in a strong position because she can't hurt me. I'll remind her which side her bread is buttered. I'm not letting her wreck your home and steal your husband. I'll see her dead first.'

Vic tensed, his eyes gleaming.

'So don't you worry,' Howard continued. 'Best to leave it tonight, anyhow. Gives me time.'

'Time?' She handed him back the glass.

'To work out what I can do.'

'I worked out the only thing I could do,' she sighed. 'I came to do it.'

'You're not getting on your knees to Freda,' Howard told her emphatically. 'She should be on *her* knees begging *your* pardon.'

'Why should she beg? She's on top.'

'Not in *this* house, she isn't! She is my wife. And, with the little work she gets these days, dependant on me.'

'That's the bit I don't understand,' she told him.

'What don't you understand?'

'What does she think you'll do when you find out? For a woman with no independence, she's behaving very independently . . . Almost as if *you* didn't exist . . .'

A sudden roar of music from the T.V. reminded them of Vic's presence. Mrs. Webb ceased her speculations at once.

'What the hell — ?' Howard snapped in exasperation.

'Sorry, sir.'

'Just *leave* the damn thing. Do it tomorrow!'

'Fairly got it fixed now, sir,' Vic said.

Mrs. Webb rose to leave. Howard stood up.

'I'll call you tomorrow.'

'Thank you. Get her to say where he is. I won't feel quite so bad if I just know that.'

Howard followed her to the door. 'She'll say more than that by the time I've finished with her.'

Mrs. Webb stopped and turned to him. 'Please! He's to blame as well. It takes two. Remember that, won't you?'

'I'll try to,' Howard grunted. They reached the door. 'Sure you're O.K. now?'

'A little walk and I'll be fine. Thank you for everything.'

Howard, about to open the door, stopped suddenly. 'One thing!'

'Yes?'

'We can't say which way this thing might go. I mean, the legal gents may take over.'

'Yes?' Vaguely.

'So, let no one know that you were here tonight. All right?'

'If you think it best.'

Howard opened the door. 'I'll show you

out the side door.'

'Thank you.'

As they both went out, Howard shouted back into the room: 'Vic! Don't go for a moment. I haven't got my key.'

Vic, grave-faced and deep in thought, left off his pretence at servicing the T.V. set. Whistling, he wandered over to the money again. He handled it again, enviously; then he picked up the slip of paper and looked at it.

'Hundred and ninety quid!' He clicked his mouth in happy speculation, and put the slip of paper back.

He went quickly to the little jug on the sideboard, and took out the back-gate key. Then he went to the garden window, drew aside the curtain, and unbolted the window, redrawing the curtain again. From the distance he heard the sound of a door being shut, and Howard's returning footsteps. Quickly, Vic dodged back to the T.V. and resumed fiddling with it.

Howard returned, slamming the door, evidence that he was in a filthy temper. He helped himself to a drink and stood there, grim and staring, thinking of Freda and her wickedness.

Vic watched him carefully, thinking of something quite different. 'Will she be all right, sir?' he asked.

'Eh?' Howard gave a start, becoming aware of the other's presence. 'Oh, yes, she'll be all right . . . By the way, thank you for your help. Er . . . have a drink?'

'Thank you, sir. A beer, please, if you have one.'

As Howard poured him a glass of beer, Vic walked slowly but deliberately over to where Howard was standing.

'Nasty little turn she had, sir,' he commented. 'Kind of upset, wasn't she?'

'Yes . . . yes, she was.' Howard snapped out of his preoccupation. 'How are you getting on with that thing?' He indicated the T.V.

Vic came to a point where the metal figure was to his right hand — as at his earlier rehearsal with Freda. He stopped, watching, as Howard finished the pouring of the beer. 'Would you like to see it working, sir?'

Howard gave him the glass of beer. Vic

accepted the drink with his left hand. Like his other hand, it was still gloved. 'No, I'll take your word for it,' he said, turning back to the sideboard to pick up his own drink. He raised it. 'Cheers.'

'Cheers, sir.'

Howard went over to his desk, and, taking a pound note off the pile, turned and approached Vic. 'Put that in your pocket.'

Slightly puzzled, Vic accepted the note.

'Nobody must know that lady was here tonight,' Howard said levelly.

'You can trust me, Mr. Nutting,' Vic assured him. 'I mean, there's no need to . . .'

'That's all right.' Howard returned to his desk, and began putting the money into a large envelope. 'Bingo money,' he explained, aware of Vic's curious gaze. 'To go in the porter's safe when I leave. But I can fiddle a quid!' He laughed.

Vic laughed too, but it died rather mirthlessly as he saw that the money was going out of sight. He went over to the T.V. with his beer as Howard sealed the envelope.

Abruptly, Howard gave way to the angry thoughts that were racing in his head, slapping the envelope down in anger. 'Always the way, isn't it?' he muttered. Vic gave a sympathetic grunt of enquiry. 'The nicest people are served the dirtiest tricks!'

'I guess you're right, sir.' Vic nodded. 'I ... er ... I couldn't help hearing ... some of it, sir. If you'll excuse me saying so, she seemed a real nice lady.'

'You thought so, too?' Howard's words were quickly uttered, betraying his feelings.

Vic nodded sagely. 'And I size up people pretty quick, sir.'

'Yes. The dirtiest tricks.' Howard gulped at his drink and frowned. 'The hell is ... what can she do about it?'

Vic gave a calculating smile. 'You promised to get something worked out, sir. I heard you.'

'Quite true. I did.' Howard shrugged. 'But what?'

'That lady was right, you know.' Vic's tone was insinuating.

'Right?'

'About it being . . . too late for reasoning.' Vic paused as Howard gave him a searching look. 'Women know more about these things than we do, sir. And she said . . . it's too late to reason.' He smiled, appearing to make up his mind about something. Howard was staring at him, sensing some mystery.

'Now the lady's gone, sir, there's something you'd better know.'

'About what?'

'About Mrs. Nutting, sir.'

'What about her?' Howard asked sharply.

Vic spoke uneasily. 'I'll be taking a great risk in telling you. But I must tell you . . . to ease my conscience.'

'What the . . . ?'

'I very nearly did something tonight, sir . . . that I'd have regretted till the end of my days.'

'What was that?' Howard asked quickly. His tone betrayed that he was becoming worried.

There was a long pause, then:

'Before I tell you, I must ask your

promise not to hand me over to the police.'

Howard frowned. 'Why should I do that?'

'Because the information I'm about to give you should be in their hands . . . ' Vic explained slowly. 'But you may prefer to keep it to yourself and . . . act on it.'

'Act on it?'

Vic spread his hands. 'It might suggest . . . a course of conduct — on your part — that would restore Mr. Webb to his wife.'

Howard narrowed his eyes. 'Information that does that would be welcome, Vic. Out with it!'

Vic hesitated, still cautious. 'First, your promise.'

'Yes, yes . . . ' Howard was becoming impatient.

'That what I reveal, whether you believe it or not, you will allow me to walk out of this flat a free man.'

'I promise,' Howard said briefly. He looked at his watch. 'And hurry; I've got a dinner to attend this evening.'

'What I tell you won't improve your

appetite,' Vic said dryly. 'Mr. Nutting, you've had one shock tonight. You've got two more to come.'

'Where from?'

'Same place. Your wife.'

'You know my wife?' Howard tightened his lips.

Vic nodded complacently. 'Better than you do, perhaps.'

'You're not a T.V. repairman, are you?' Howard demanded. Vic shook his head. 'Then how did you know we were expecting one?'

'All that in a moment, sir.' Vic was in no hurry now that he was sure he had Howard's undivided attention.

'All that *now*, if you don't mind!' Howard snapped impatiently. 'You know, when I opened that door to you . . . ' He pointed to it. ' . . . you seemed . . . wrong. It was the way you came in. You've been here before?'

Vic nodded. 'Once,' he admitted. 'Yesterday. By request. Your wife phoned me.'

There was a long pause.

'Look here,' Howard demanded. 'Who

are you, and *what* are you?'

'I do jobs about the house. I advertise in shops.'

'A male domestic?'

'On my card, I say: 'Fit young man. Anything legal.' . . . Women call me.' He paused suggestively. 'Are you with me?'

'I'm ahead of you,' Howard snapped. 'So . . . my wife hired you, did she?'

'Yes, sir.'

'God in heaven!'

Vic smiled at the other's wrong assumption. '*Not* as a professional lover,' he assured him.

Howard's eyes widened. 'Then as what?

'A professional murderer.'

Howard tensed, horrified at this unexpected revelation. 'To murder Mrs. Webb?'

'No, sir. To murder *you*!'

3

Howard half-turned towards the nearby desk, without once taking his eyes off Vic. He moistened his suddenly-dry lips, rubbed the corners of his mouth with his fingers.

'No need to be afraid of me, sir.' Vic smiled.

Howard puffed out his cheeks. 'Don't worry, I am not.' He was doing some fast thinking. 'Vic, I made you a promise.'

'Yes, Mr. Nutting.'

'Then . . . would you like to finish your beer?'

Vic did so, and was about to return the glass to the sideboard when Howard indicated the nearby settee table. 'On *that* table will do.' Vic complied, smiling. 'Now, pick up your little bag.'

Vic crossed to the T.V. and picked up his tool-bag. He stood looking at Howard expectantly.

'Goodnight, Vic. I shall watch from this

window. If I don't see you cross the road and go right away from these flats, I shall call the cops. Although I think it's a *doctor* you need.'

'No need to be insulting, sir,' Vic muttered, nettled. 'There's gratitude! I do you a favour, put you wise to your wife . . . and I'm insulted and shown the door.'

Vic had not moved. He had not yet played all his cards.

'I haven't told you the half of it yet, anyway. The best was still to come.' He shrugged. 'However, if you're the type that can't take it, I'll . . . push off.'

He moved towards the door, then looked over his shoulder. 'And . . . thank you for inviting me. Goodnight, Mr. Nutting. I'll be . . . reading about you.'

Vic crossed to the door, and was about to open it when Howard spoke sharply.

'Wait!'

Vic stopped.

'I'll hear the rest.' Howard indicated a hard chair at the side of the fireplace. 'Sit in that chair. I want to hear what else you have to say.'

Vic hesitated. 'Your promise still holds?'

'It still holds.'

'O.K.' Vic went to the chair indicated, and laid his bag down alongside it. Seating himself, he began to put his newly-conceived plan into operation.

'Well, when I first met your wife and talked to her, she felt her way a bit at first . . . then she comes out with her proposition.'

'Which was?' Howard's tone was grim.

'To bump you off. For five hundred quid.'

'Five hundred?' Howard frowned. 'But . . . ?'

'Her life savings, so she said.'

'I see. And you consented?'

'Yes.'

Howard's expression changed. 'What kind of man are you?'

'Don't judge me too quick, sir,' Vic said complacently. 'You see, I didn't know then what I know now.'

'Oh?'

'*She's* the one wants bumping off! Your wife — not you!'

'Never mind that!' Howard snapped. 'Tell me what you were to do.'

'Her plan was foolproof, sir, perfect . . . oh yes, very clever!'

'You surprise me!' Howard smiled bitterly. 'I've never found that inventiveness was her strong point.' He shrugged. 'Go on with your story.'

'Her plan would have gone through if it hadn't been for Mrs. Webb,' Vic resumed. 'You owe your life to her, sir.'

'How?'

'You see, sir, I was to bash you . . . ' Vic pointed to the metal figure. ' . . . with that thing, as soon as I was in and the door shut.'

'You call that clever?' Howard was appalled.

'Fooled me, anyhow!'

'Fooled you?'

' "Have no conversation with him," she said. "It will weaken your resolve." I see now what she was up to. Why she wanted it done in such a hurry. She was afraid I'd get on to the truth about you.'

'The truth about me?' Howard frowned in puzzlement.

'Yeah. That you're an ordinary decent bloke, and not what she said you were.'

'And what was that?'

'Are you ready for your third shock?'

Howard waved a hand dismissively. 'I am ready for anything. What was it?'

'Quote . . . 'A man so foul, a creature so disgusting, that the world would be a much better place without him.''

'If I'm not being unduly curious, *what* was I?'

Vic's answer astounded Howard. 'A sexual monstrosity . . . a seducer of boys.'

Howard goggled, speechless. He left his desk and took a few faltering steps towards Vic, looked at him acutely, then turned away with a long, horrified exhalation. 'No!' He managed to find his way back to his desk. He was clearly stunned.

'Can you imagine how I feel, sir?' Vic went on. 'Almost tricked into murdering an innocent man? I *believed* her lies! Believed all that about you. That was what decided me . . . made my job easy, you might say . . . '

'And but for Mrs. Webb . . . ?' Howard whispered.

'I'd never have slept again,' Vic said frankly. 'If I'd ever found out, that is. But then, I wouldn't ever have found out, would I? If I'd done it? She knew that. Dead men don't talk. No wonder she said, 'Do it straight away and send the signal.''

'What signal?'

''Mission accomplished.'' Vic pointed to the phone. 'She's sitting by the phone box at her club.'

'Then she'll be wondering why she hasn't got her signal.'

'She *has* got it.'

Howard gave a little start. 'That odd call you made.' Vic nodded. 'Optimist, weren't you?'

'It was still to do. Mrs. Webb was just going. I was still believing all that about you,' Vic admitted.

'When did you stop believing?'

'Later, when you were with Mrs. Webb, and . . . '

'And what?'

'Well, now I know you, I can see you're not that sort.'

'So,' Howard mused, 'at this point

. . . she's sitting by that phone box, sipping her grin. Probably celebrating her widowhood, all to herself.'

'No doubt about that, sir.'

''I'll wear my black tonight,' she said.' Howard scowled as he realised the significance of his wife's parting words. 'What else? She believes me dead. What happens from now? She said she's coming back at nine to see something.'

Vic nodded soberly. 'Your dead body. She pays me, and that's me over. Technical evidence will establish you've been dead two hours. And you spoke to the porter over the buzzer *after* she left.'

'Her alibi,' Howard whispered. He saw now how everything was fitting into place in the web of treachery.

'She won't need an alibi with the story she's been rehearsing,' Vic said frankly. 'She's going to make *True Life* look like Beatrix Potter. My God! Does she play safe!'

'What's she going to tell them?'

'The lot!' Vic spread his hands. 'You're a sexual Jekyll and Hyde. But it's all Hyde and no Jekyll. Her marriage is a sham, a cover for your sex lark. Dependent on you, she must bear her humiliation in silent suffering.'

'God!'

'You pick up young men and bring them home . . . been doing it for years. There was one tonight as soon as her back was turned — Terry. But he wouldn't play. He was so outraged at your suggestion that he just hit you with . . . ' He pointed again to the metal figure. ' . . . the first thing he could find, and then he ran out.' He nodded towards the garden window.

'They'd very likely believe it,' Howard whispered, appalled.

'The good old British public would swallow it whole,' Vic agreed. 'And if there was the odd Doubting Thomas, she still had her heavy stuff to bring up . . . the Boys' Camp.'

'That as well?

'It was that decided me.'

'Decided you?'

'I'm one of the British public, too.'

'Yes, of course,' Howard said. 'She

would count on that. I'm sorry to be so dense. This isn't really my subject.'

'May I leave this chair, Mr. Nutting?' Vic asked at length. Howard looked at him quickly, alert to danger, but relaxed, having decided there was nothing for him to fear from Vic now. 'I want to show you something.'

'Go ahead.' Howard waved a hand.

Vic went over and retrieved the key of Howard's dresser drawer from the sideboard, then proceeded to Howard's bedroom door.

'May I?'

'Yes.'

'She planted evidence of your double life . . . ' Vic told him, going into the bedroom, and returning at once with the drawer. ' . . . for the police to find.'

Howard looked at the items in the drawer.

'Your secret hidey-hole,' Vic commented. Howard looked briefly at the pictures. 'Filthy pictures to excite your victim.'

'They're not mine,' Howard said angrily. 'They were found here after a party. I *told* her to throw them out.' He put them back. 'She'd do this to me!'

Vic pointed to Howard's bedroom. 'Your seduction parlour, complete with cotton wool in the keyhole. And a bolt on the door.'

'Bolt? That's never been used. It was there when we came. Some old maid lived here.' Howard took a closer look at the bolt. 'God! She's oiled it! She's got it to work.'

'She's a great one for detail.' Vic put the drawer back in the bedroom and came out again.

Howard said slowly: 'We're no longer man and wife . . . but I do feed her . . . I keep a roof over her head.'

Vic replaced the key, then got out the Coca-Cola glass, holding it by the extreme edge of its rim. 'This as well.'

Howard reached to take it, but Vic stopped him.

'Mustn't touch! Fingerprints! Terry's. She pinched it from Victoria Coach Station.' He got out the bottle of Coca-Cola. 'Good clean type. He drank Coca-Cola.'

'She *never* buys Coca-Cola,' Howard said.

Vic shrugged. 'Special occasion.' He put the glass and bottle away again. 'As soon as you got in tonight, you asked twice had Terry phoned.'

Howard was deeply affected by Vic's revelations of his wife's scheming. He remained silent for some time, then went down to his desk again. Vic waited, watching him intently.

A terrible resolve was growing in him. 'She's coming back at nine?'

'Yes.'

'Then get out, Vic! Get out!'

Howard's outburst took Vic by surprise. 'What are you going to do?'

'Just get out. Don't worry. I shan't report you.'

'But . . . ?'

'I want to be alone when she gets here!' Howard snapped. 'Get out.'

'Mr. Nutting, I . . . '

Howard turned to Vic agitatedly. 'Go! While you can!'

'What are you going to do?' Vic repeated his unanswered question —

though he already suspected the answer.

'What any man with a backbone would do.' Howard turned away.

Still, Vic lingered. 'If you'll excuse me saying so . . . '

'Go!' Howard roared. 'Before I . . . '

'All right,' said Vic hastily. 'I'll go. And thank you for letting me.' He picked up his bag and went to the door — where, however, he stopped again. Instead of leaving, he turned to stand, watching the motionless figure of Howard at the desk.

It was some time before Vic considered it safe to speak again.

'Right. You kill her. Any man with a backbone *would*, as you say. She's not fit to live. We both know that. But nobody else knows that . . . ' He paused, then added heavily: 'You could get a twenty-year stretch.'

'I'd cherish every minute of it,' Howard said stubbornly.

'You'd be rotting with regret before the trial started,' Vic pointed out.

'She's not fit to live. You just said so yourself!'

'Agreed.'

'She should be dead.'

'Agreed again.' Vic took a deep breath, and began to play his hand. 'But she's not worth rotting in prison for. Are you going to let her do that to you? That's worse than what she got me here to do to you.' He paused to give time for his words to sink in. 'She's caused enough suffering already. Your way, she'll cause another dose . . . after she's dead . . . to you.'

Howard was visibly wavering. Vic went on:

'You're a writer . . . of comedy. Oh, you could still write in prison. But not comedy. Oh, no, comedy would be right out. You'd have to write about . . . the cancer of the soul . . . stuff like that.'

'She must die,' Howard muttered.

'But you must be at your dinner when she does so.' Howard flashed him a glance. 'I'd like to get even with her. Because of her, I might have murdered you. I'll thank God till the end of my days that I didn't. But here's my chance to . . . atone . . . for my lunacy in believing her.'

Howard was now wavering with indecision, and Vic pressed home his viewpoint. 'I feel I'm entitled to some consideration. I never asked to be brought here. She phoned me, out of the blue, wanted a job doing . . . said the world would be a better place when it was done.'

'You were to receive five hundred, you said?'

'Yes, sir.'

'But did she give you nothing on account?'

'No.'

Howard frowned. 'Surely . . . ?'

'I was to take the Bingo money,' Vic explained.

'So you've had nothing for all your trouble. I'm sorry.'

'That's soon put right.' Vic had been building up to this moment. 'For here's a similar job. Let me do her . . . on the same terms.'

Howard shook his head slowly. 'I'd be paying twice.'

'How?'

'By paying you, and by foregoing the pleasure of doing it myself.'

'You'd get instead the pleasure of knowing she's dead and that they can't get you for it.' Vic paused as Howard's face showed his indecision. 'And Mrs. Webb gets her husband back,' he added. 'You promised her you'd work something out. I've done it for you.'

'Oh, *God!*' Howard was clearly tormented with indecision. Vic continued to press him.

'You'll have to decide soon, sir.' He pointed dramatically. 'She'll be through that door before long to view your body.'

His words had their desired effect in rousing Howard to a decision.

'Vic, you're right. She's not worth rotting in prison for. She's not worth losing a night's sleep for . . . But she must die.'

'Yes, sir. We settled *that* ten minutes ago,' Vic said patiently.

'You'd do it?'

'Didn't I say?'

'Same price?'

'O.K . . . ' Vic's tone hardened. 'But I want half the money now.'

'I've no money tonight,' Howard said,

momentarily disconcerted. Then he brightened. 'There's the Bingo money . . . '

'Of course.'

Howard blew out his cheeks. 'What a bit of luck!' He unsealed the envelope, extracting a bundle of a hundred pounds, and handing it to Vic. 'I can fiddle a hundred now. There you are, Vic.'

'And the rest?' Vic pressed, eagerly. 'The four hundred?'

Howard carefully resealed the envelope. 'Give me a couple of weeks to get it.' He reflected for a few moments, then: 'I'll advertise a radio for sale . . . *Evening News* . . . Saturday week. Come at nine o'clock, side door.'

'O.K. But don't forget . . . I'm trusting you, Mr. Nutting.'

'As I am you.'

Vic held out his hand. 'Shall we shake on that?'

They shook hands to seal their bargain.

'Right! Now let us get organised.' Howard looked at his watch. 'I'm late. Talk while I'm dressing.' Howard dodged into his bedroom and emerged with his shoes, tie and jacket. He began to put them on while continuing talking to Vic. 'What happens?'

'Simple, sir. Burglar breaks in. She disturbs him. She starts screaming, he panics, and . . . Bob's your Uncle.'

Howard shook his head. 'Not madly original. We must do better than that.'

Both men thought for a moment. Then suddenly Vic seemed to have another inspiration. 'God! It's sticking out a mile!'

'Don't get you.'

Vic pointed to the money on the desk. 'That money's from the camp, you say?' At Howard's nod, he continued: 'Those boys know it's here?'

'They do.'

'And money is the one thing they're short of, I'll bet.' Vic smiled.

'They haven't any.'

Vic nodded complacently. 'Well, there you are. They hitch-hike here, wait till you leave, and get in. She surprises them, and they have to do her because she'd know them again.'

'Don't be daft!' Howard snapped. 'My boys wouldn't do *that*! My boys are not *crooks*, you know!'

'But, surely they . . . ?'

'*Were* crooks, perhaps. But down there, free and happy, no bolts or bars, nobody shouting at them, they're not crooks, they're . . . '

'Just happy kids again,' Vic finished disconsolately. 'I'd forgotten that. You've forgotten something else, too.'

'What?'

'Isn't it obvious? The phoney T.V. man does it. He could have seen the money while he was pretending to service the set.'

'Good God, yes.' Vic watched as Howard crossed to the garden window and unbolted it. 'He unbolts the garden window, leaves, waits in the street till I go; then walks round into the lane, gets over the garden wall and in. He comes back, etcetera, etcetera — all that's the same!'

Vic nodded in satisfaction. 'That's it then.'

'Right, Vic. Get your bag,' Howard instructed him. 'Make sure the porter sees you go out.' As Vic frowned, Howard added: 'You know why?'

'I get it. Because he didn't see me come in.'

'Too true! And I want a reliable witness that there *was* a T.V. man. I'll just make sure he's there.' Going over to the buzzer, Howard dialled and waited. 'Just as long as he sees a stranger with a tool-bag. Put on an accent to say 'Goodnight' to him,

Howard got a reply, and spoke into the buzzer. 'Porter . . . ? Nutting here . . . What time have you got? Mine's stopped . . . Thank you. Will you be there for the next five minutes? I've some money to go in the safe . . . Thank you.' He hung up, and turned back to Vic. 'He's there. Get cracking, Vic.'

'Yes, sir.'

'And when you heave yourself over the wall — ' Howard pointed into the garden. ' — be sure to leave plenty of scratches . . . evidence of entry.'

'O.K., sir. By the way . . . ' Vic pointed to his beer glass. 'My glass wants washing. And Mrs. Webb's too.'

'Of course. I'll take them.' Howard collected the three glasses and went into the kitchen with them.

Vic took the garden key out of his pocket, looked at it, and put it back. Going over to the garden window, he bolted it, leaving the curtain drawn. Then, picking up his bag, he went out, shutting the door behind him.

Presently Howard came back with the cleaned glasses and put them away. He took Vic's beer bottle and went into the kitchen with it. Returning straight away, he went over to the buzzer and dialled. 'Porter . . . ? Mr. Nutting . . . call me a cab, will you . . . ? Yes, straight away. I'm late . . . '

Howard donned his dinner jacket before going into the bathroom and coming out with a medicine glass containing his buttonhole flower. He wiped away the surplus water on the flower with a paper tissue, which he threw in the paper bin. Securing the flower in his buttonhole, he left the glass on the sideboard.

Next he got his overcoat and scarf from the rack at the hall door and put them on. He checked that he had his cigarettes, lighter, spectacles, cash, pocketbook and latchkey. Crossing to his desk, he pocketed the seated envelope.

Howard turned as he heard a light tapping on the garden window. Drawing the curtain, he saw that Vic was standing outside. He unbolted the garden window and admitted him into the room.

'Leave this unbolted now. All right?'

'O.K.' Vic was panting a little from exertion, and his overalls and shoes showed stains consistent with his having clambered over a wall. 'Made some smashing scratches, sir. They'll think the T.V. man was very overweight!'

'Right. You're on your own now, Vic. O.K.?'

'O.K. sir.'

Howard went to hall door, then turned. 'Till Saturday week.'

'Saturday week it is, sir.'

Howard gave him a thumbs-up sign. 'Good luck!'

Vic nodded, smiling grimly. 'Thank you, sir. Enjoy your evening.'

'Thank you, Vic. And the same to you.' With that, Howard left, shutting the hall door behind him.

Vic checked the time, then briskly set about putting his plan into operation. First, he subdued the lighting by taking out the settee-table light. Then be began to gather up cushions, pillows, rolled-up newspapers, and a pair of Howard's shoes from his bedroom. Quickly, he began to bulk them together to make up the rough shape of a body on the floor below the settee.

He covered it with a rug, and with Howard's shoes peeping out from under it at the end nearest the desk, it looked quite realistic at first glance from a distance. He confirmed this himself by looking at it from the hall door, then altered the position so that only the feet would be seen from such a viewpoint.

Finally, he laid the metal ornament — the 'murder weapon' — near the 'body'.

Satisfied with this work, Vic crossed to the coat rack, from where he selected one of Freda's scarves. He tried it for length and for strength, then set about rehearsing what he intended to do.

With the scarf firmly gripped in both

hands, he went over and stood at the side of the hall door, so that the opening of it would conceal him.

Reaching over, he opened the door, pretending that Freda was entering. He followed with his eye her progress from the open doorway to the 'body'.

Suddenly slamming the door, he darted behind her, whipping the scarf over her head and drawing her violently to him. He whispered to himself, 'Now, Mrs. Nutting . . . the four hundred . . . or there *will* be a murder.'

Suddenly, he stopped the rehearsal. He was not satisfied with it. After a few moments' further thought, he hit upon another idea.

Going over to it, he sat in the desk chair, elbows on knees, staring at the 'body'. He imagined getting himself into an emotional state, contemplating the awful thing he had done. His eyes darted suddenly towards the door, as though someone was entering.

He imagined that Freda had come into the room, and was standing looking at him.

He would avoid looking at her directly, and pretend that he was having some sort of breakdown. He could simulate hysterical muttering along the lines of:

'No, no! You look! You look! I can't . . . I can't, I tell you!'

He pictured Freda going forward and bending to lift the rug.

As before, he darted forward like lightning, getting the scarf over her head and drawing her to him. Savagely, he thought: 'Now, Mrs. Nutting, the four hundred, if you please — or there *will* be murder.'

He stopped rehearsing. He was happier with his second idea. Yes, he would settle for that.

Suddenly he tensed, registering discomfort at an urgent call of nature. His nervous state, probably accentuated by the beer he had drunk, necessitated an immediate visit to the bathroom, tugging at his gloves.

A minute later, after flushing, he came back into the room, putting his gloves back on as he did so.

He gave a start as the clock in the room

116

began to chime, very softly, the hour of nine. He grabbed the scarf again, and took up his position in the desk chair. He helped himself into character again, rehearsing his muttering: 'No! No! I can't look, I tell you! I'm afraid, I tell you! Afraid of his eyes! And what I'll see in them . . . '

He stopped abruptly as a nearby church clock — cracked, harsh, and unmelodious — started to chime the hour of nine. Vic fought the impulse to light a cigarette to calm his jagged nerves by going into character again.

' . . . ashamed, I tell you . . . ashamed of what I've done. I can't look at him . . . not again!'

He stopped muttering to himself. All was deadly quiet as he tensely awaited Freda's return, due at any moment.

The more distant and stately chimes of Big Ben began to sound in the night, marking the hour of nine. *God! Would that cow ever come home?*

Big Ben was still chiming as the outside hall light came on, and a key was put into the lock . . .

4

It was several hours later that night, at the home of Howard and Freda Nutting. All the lights were on and the curtains drawn — except at the garden window.

The garden window was wide open and several police officers were working at the bottom of the terrace steps, augmenting the light from the house with torches as they scoured the garden and examined the wall at the far end.

The low murmur of their voices could be heard inside the house, where a dead body — completely covered by a rug — was lying on the floor below the settee. It was in much the same position as had been the crude dummy that Vic had left earlier that night.

Detective Inspector Robin, C.I.D., in charge of the local Police Division, was at the door to the hall, trying the lock and examining the woodwork around it. Robin was middle-aged, and although of only medium height, he was solidly built, almost bull-like, and very nearly as pugnacious when aroused. Bushy eyebrows above a short nose and prominent chin completed a face that typified dogged persistency.

Straightening up from his examination of the lock, he checked the time and gave a puzzled frown. He went over to the buzzer and dialled once. He received a quick reply that caused him to frown again.

'Garage . . . ? No, no, I don't want the garage. I'm sorry . . . ' Robin hung up in exasperation. Going over to the garden window, he called down from the top of the terrace to the officers working in the garden. 'Edwards!'

'Yes, Inspector?' an answering voice sounded from the gloom outside.

'How do I get the front lobby, the porter, on this confounded buzzer thing?' Robin demanded testily.

'Dial five, sir, for the porter. Dial five.'

'Thanks,' Robin grunted. He was coming away from the terrace when he halted, and turned to speak again to the officers working in the garden.

'I don't think you can do much good there tonight, you men. It's too dark. Best to leave it till daylight.'

'We're just finishing, sir,' a voice answered.

Back inside the living room, Robin operated the buzzer again, this time getting his man.

'Porter . . . ? Is my sergeant there . . . ? Put him on, will you . . . ? Any sign of this man Nutting yet . . . ? Taking his time, isn't he . . . ? Yes, of course . . . '

Hanging up, he moved away, his expression immensely thoughtful.

He glanced briefly at the body, then interested himself in the scarf — the same item that Vic had selected earlier in the evening. It was now hanging over the back of the desk chair.

He went over to it, not with an air of discovery, but as though he was reaffirming an opinion he already held.

Picking it up, he tested its strength with one or two jerks. Taking it over to the desk light, he held it against the glow, examining any damage there might be to the fibres or distortion to the weave. At length, he concluded his little examination and replaced the scarf on the back of the chair.

He was about to go into the garden again when he turned at the sound of Howard Nutting hurrying in from the hall door. He appeared somewhat breathless from hurrying.

Howard stared at the Inspector standing near to the settee, regarding him keenly. He halted, clearly disconcerted. 'Oh!'

'Mr. Nutting?'

'Yes.' Howard nodded slowly.

'I am Detective Inspector Robin, C.I.D., in charge of this division.'

'Yes. I see . . . '

Howard, from where he stood just inside the hall door, could not see the rug-covered body. It was hidden from his view by the settee and the inspector. He began to divest himself of his overcoat.

'You got our message, sir?' Robin asked, as Howard began to dart glances around the room.

'Yes, Inspector.'

'I was beginning to wonder,' Robin said, dryly.

'There was a spot of rain . . . I couldn't get a taxi,' Howard explained.

Robin smiled. 'Of course. I'm not criticising. They should have asked to speak to you personally.'

Howard spoke anxiously: 'The head waiter brought me a message that was a bit vague, I must say. There'd been a burglar in my home . . . resulting in an accident.' He frowned. 'He said that was all they told him. Very worrying — but at least I knew that my wife wasn't at home.'

Robin shook his head. 'I'm afraid, sir,' he said gravely, 'she *was* at home.'

Howard's expression showed an increased anxiety.

'I must ask you to prepare yourself for a shock, Mr. Nutting. There's been murder done here tonight.' Robin moved aside deliberately, allowing Howard full view of the rug-covered body for the first time.

Grave-faced and now alarmed, Howard moved to the rug-covered body, and bent over. He was about to lift the corner of the rug when Freda suddenly emerged from out of her bedroom.

'Howard!'

Howard froze. He straightened and turned to regard his wife as she hurried over to him, very tear-stained and upset. She threw her arms around him and clung to him. Robin watched the tableau impassively.

'Oh, my darling, thank God, you've got here! Thank God you've come!' For a second or two she wept against him, then looked up as he gently disengaged himself. 'Oh, God! Poor Mrs. Webb!'

Howard gave a horrified start at the mention of the woman's name, and quickly bent down again to lift the rug . . .

The next moment, the bedroom door opened, and Mrs. Webb came out on the arm of a police matron. She was utterly subdued, and clearly deeply upset.

'Mrs. Webb!' Robin exclaimed, his voice at once sympathetic.

Howard straightened up quickly, and he and Mrs. Webb looked at each other for a second, neither showing recognition.

Robin moved a step or two to towards her. 'Madam, you promised to rest until the car got here . . . '

'Never mind the car,' she said tonelessly. 'I'll walk.'

At the sound of a bell, Robin opened the hall door and looked out at another police officer standing there. 'Yes?'

'Car's here now, sir.'

Robin turned, 'The car is here, Mrs. Webb. Better if you were to take it.'

'Thank you.'

Howard had now lifted the corner of the rug and looked at the body curiously. He let the rug drop quickly, his expression puzzled.

The inspector escorted Mrs. Webb out of the room, giving her over to the impassive police matron. 'Try and get some sleep, Mrs. Webb.'

She looked at him with tear-filled eyes. 'Sleep . . . ?' Her voice was edged with bitterness.

'The matron will go along with you now,' he said gently. 'I'll come and see how you are in the morning.'

Mrs. Webb passed out with the police

matron. The Inspector closed the door, and approached Howard. 'Did you know the dead man, sir?'

'No, Inspector.'

'Ever seen him before?'

'No.' Howard shook his head firmly. 'It's that lady's husband, isn't it?'

'What makes you think so?' Robin asked sharply.

'Why, her distress, of course.'

'I see. Yes, it is — or was — her husband . . . ' Robin paused, then rapped out: 'Do you know the lady?'

'No, Inspector.'

'Have you ever seen her before?' Robin persisted.

'No.' Howard managed to keep his voice steady as he lied.

Robin let the matter drop, changing the subject of his questioning. 'So it was at the Connaught Rooms you were dining tonight?'

'I was there, yes.'

'We had a bit of a job tracking you down,' Robin remarked. 'They said you'd gone to your club.'

'I went to my club *first*,' Howard

explained. 'Then on from there.'

Robin nodded. 'Your club is Kerby's in Fitzmore Street, so the porter said.'

'Yes.'

'What time did you leave here, sir?'

'Eight-thirtyish. The porter called me a cab, I had a drink at my club — a quick one, as we were late. Then on to the dinner with a friend.' Howard looked at the impassive Robin anxiously. 'Do you want his name, Inspector?'

Robin shook his head and smiled. 'No, no.'

'The speeches were just starting when the head waiter brought your message . . . ' Howard paused, and added plaintively: 'What's been going on, Inspector?'

Robin shrugged apologetically. 'Oh . . . we've a good bit of work to do yet to find out everything. You're going to have a disturbed night, I'm afraid. We'll be as quiet as we can, naturally.'

'But what happened?'

'Your wife called us,' Robin said, glancing at Freda, who was now sitting, looking distinctly uncomfortable, in the chair at the desk. 'She came home and found a burglar helping himself. He tried to strangle her. Mr. Webb, who happened to be passing, came to her assistance. There was a struggle for a gun . . . yours, I'm told.' He indicated the body. 'With this result.'

'And the burglar?'

'Made off through the garden, apparently.'

Howard frowned. 'What was Mrs. Webb doing here?'

'Your wife says she came in after the shooting.' Robin's voice was bland.

Freda looked up, angry and tearful. 'She did. And when she saw him lying there . . . shot . . . she thought *I'd* done it!'

'Why should she think that?' Howard asked sharply.

'Her husband left her!' Freda cried agitatedly. 'Went to live with some floozy! Then she found he was living here . . . upstairs . . . so she thought I was the . . . woman.' Her face twisted. 'Like a lunatic, she was! Accused me of being in love with him. That was plain stupid.' She looked at Howard for support. 'If I loved him, I wouldn't shoot him, would I?'

To her annoyance, her husband remained expressionless.

'Didn't Mrs. Webb see the burglar?' he asked.

'No. Only me! And poor Mr. Webb!' Freda broke into tears again.

Robin moved towards Freda. 'There now, madam, that doesn't help.'

'I'm sorry,' she blubbed, and made an effort to calm herself.

'You said you'd check, madam,' Robin reminded her, 'and let us know what he took of yours, if anything.'

'I'm afraid to look.' Freda sniffed.

Robin raised an eyebrow. 'Afraid to look?'

'At my jewel box. I just know I'll find it empty.'

'I'll take a look,' Howard said decisively. 'It's got to be faced, Freda.'

Robin gave him a grateful glance. 'Thank you, sir.'

As Howard crossed the room to Freda's bedroom, she started to cry again. 'I know it'll be empty!'

Robin touched her lightly on the shoulder, softened his tone. 'You're upsetting yourself again, madam. We'll be going into all this tomorrow. So don't you think it would be better now, if you go back to your room and lie down?'

'I can't rest if I do,' Freda demurred.

'Don't worry about that,' Robin said. 'When the doctor comes, I'll get him to give you something.'

Freda sniffed. 'Thank you.'

The next moment, Howard came out of Freda's bedroom, carrying her jewel box. She turned to him quickly. 'Has he — ?'

'It's all here, as far as I can see,' Howard answered, placing the jewel box on the desk, so that she could examine it herself and determine whether anything was missing.

Robin watched her whilst she examined the contents. 'Well, madam?'

Freda didn't answer, went on looking at her pieces. Robin sighed, and turned to her husband. 'I'd be glad to know if he took anything of yours, sir.'

'Certainly, Inspector.' Howard hurried

into his own bedroom.

Freda finally finished her rummaging in her jewel box. She looked up to where Robin was patiently waiting. 'No. It's all here, thank God.'

'Good,' Robin murmured, and began moving away from her. He halted when Freda suddenly remarked: 'He'd see that money on this desk, you see . . . '

Robin frowned. 'Pardon?'

'That T.V. man!' Freda went on earnestly. 'He'd see the money lying there, and . . . come back. My husband is very careless about money.'

Howard came out of his bedroom, smiling. 'He seems to have overlooked me, Inspector.'

'That's what you think!' Freda snapped, pointing to the desk. 'He's taken all that money.'

Howard stared blankly. 'All *what* money?'

Robin glanced at him in surprise. 'Your wife says you had a large sum of money in the house.'

Howard looked at his wife, smiled faintly. 'Not a large sum, dear. And he can't have taken *that*. I put it in the porter's safe.' An expression of shocked surprise crossed Freda's face. Howard turned to Robin. 'I'm always very careful about money, Inspector. Never leave temptation lying about.' He went over to the garden window, and looked back over his shoulder. 'He got out this way, you say?'

'Not much doubt about that,' Robin told him. 'It's how he got *in* that puzzles us.'

Howard stepped out on to the terrace, looking for a second at what was going on in the garden before continuing down the steps towards the policemen who were packing up their equipment.

Freda looked at the Inspector, whose expression was now impassive. 'He posed as a T.V. man. That's how he got in.'

Robin frowned slightly. 'I told you, madam. The porter says he saw no T.V. man.'

'How could he?' Freda cried dismissively. 'Over at The Grapes most of the evening . . . lifting his elbow. That man could have just walked in.' She turned to regard her husband as he wandered back inside from the terrace. 'That's what happened, Howard. He saw that money. Saw you were going out. He unbolted that window — ' She pointed to it. ' — then he left. Waited outside till *you* left. Then into the lane and over the wall. That's how he got in, dear.'

Howard spoke deliberately: 'How *who* got in, Freda?'

Freda looked at him in surprise. 'The T.V. man, of course!'

'T.V. man? *What* T.V. man?' Howard was smiling thinly.

5

It was ten o'clock the next morning. Inside the Nutting household the curtains were still drawn, sunlight peeping through them in places. Birdsong could be heard from the garden.

Freda's bedroom door opened as she emerged groggily from her bed, her dazed appearance showing evidence of the drug she had been given by the police doctor the night before. She was struggling to fix an old dressing gown round her.

Freda yawned and scratched, closing her eyes with an enormous weariness. She leant against the doorpost of her room, striving to recover.

After a moment, memory stirred, and she gave an uneasy glance around the room, afraid to find that the dead body was still there. She exhaled a long breath as she saw that it was not. Next, her curiosity focused on Howard's room door. It was closed.

She tip-toed over to it, and listened. Hearing nothing from inside, she called softly: 'Howard?'

No reply.

'Howard?' A little louder this time.

Still no reply.

Mystified, she bent to look through the keyhole, only to discover that she was unable to see anything because it had been stuffed with cotton-wool.

Cotton-wool? What was cotton-wool doing in there ... ? Suddenly she remembered. 'Oh, yes.' She frowned as she remembered more. 'Oh, God!'

She straightened up, her worry increasing. She got a cigarette, only to break off coughing after lighting it. Catching sight of the clock, she peered at it in disbelief.

'That's *never* the time!' She held the clock to her ear. 'Must be. It's going.' She looked around her unhappily. 'Sleeping till now! What did that lunatic give me, for God's sake?'

Going to the television, she prowled suspiciously around it, and discovered the plug was disconnected. Picking it up, she smiled rather grimly.

Suddenly, the hall door opened and Howard came in briskly, carrying milk, papers, letters, and a document case. Quickly, she discarded the plug. He appeared not to notice her.

'Morning, dear.' Freda went over to him, offering her cheek for the ritualistic morning peck. Instead, to her surprise, Howard merely dumped the bottle of milk into her hands, before going over to his desk and putting down the letters, papers and document case. Then he picked up the hard chair and was on his way to the hall with it when Freda found her voice again:

'Where are you taking that?'

'Into the hall.'

'I can see that,' Freda said testily. 'What for, into the hall?'

Howard did not stop. 'For the policeman to take the weight off his feet.' His answer was clipped; barely civil.

After taking the chair out, Howard returned, shutting the door behind him, and crossed to his desk.

'What's a policeman doing in our hall?' Freda demanded.

'Making sure you don't go off on your holidays.'

Freda scowled. 'That's not very funny.'

'It's early yet,' Howard said dryly. 'I shall improve.' Ignoring his wife, he went over to look at the letters on his desk.

Freda put down the milk and crossed to the window. 'They'd be better employed looking for that murderer than sitting in our hall.' She reached to open the curtains, but Howard's voice checked her.

'I should leave them drawn.'

'Why?'

Howard pointed outside. 'Murder fans! Street's full of them. If they think the flat is empty, they'll go away.'

Freda let the curtains drop back as they were, picked up the milk, and turned towards the kitchen. 'I'll get some breakfast.'

'Not for me,' Howard said briefly. 'I've had it.'

'Had it?'

'At the Berrington.'

'Berrington . . . ?'

'Hotel. I moved in last night.'

'Moved into the Berrington?' Freda looked at him dazedly. 'What for?'

'To live.'

'Just what is all this?' Freda's voice rose.

'All this, Freda,' Howard said harshly, 'is the parting of the ways.'

Freda was stunned. 'The parting of the . . . ? Just what the hell is going on in your head?'

Howard did not answer her, but calmly continued opening his letters.

Freda's eyes narrowed. 'You think Bernard Webb and me were having an affair!' she snapped. 'That's in the back of your mind, isn't it?'

'As a matter of fact,' Howard grunted, 'it's in the *front*!'

'Well, you couldn't be more wrong; and you couldn't be more bloody insulting, either.' Freda's tone was injured.

'Really?' Howard gave her a disbelieving glance.

'Bernard Webb was just a rather boring man who was pestering me to get him into show business.' Freda pouted. 'He meant nothing to me!'

137

'Where did you meet him?'

'Where everybody else meets him,' Freda said petulantly. 'In his office. He was the manager of the Sun Tan Travel Agency down the street.' She paused and looked at her husband. His expression remained sceptical. She continued with her cover-up story, mixing the truth with spin.

'He recently took part in a documentary for his firm . . . saw himself on the goggle-box . . . thought he was God's gift. I was in there getting a brochure, and happened to mention that I was in show business . . . Stupidest thing I ever did?'

'How did he come to be living upstairs?' Howard asked pointedly.

'No mystery about that, either.' Freda spread her hands. 'He drank in the same pub as the porter. Ernie has a little sideline in key money when a flat becomes empty — ' She broke off at the sound of the kettle whistling in the kitchen, and hurried to attend to it.

When she emerged, Howard had finished reading his letters, and was now looking at the papers.

Freda sipped at the coffee cup she was holding. 'What do the papers say?'

'That we have both moved out from our love nest; I to the Berrington Hotel — ' Howard smiled thinly. ' — and you to Holloway Prison.'

'What?' Freda's vice was almost a screech.

Howard shrugged. 'As good as, anyway.' He picked up a red-top. 'I'll quote: 'Mrs. Nutting left Kingston Court just before midnight in a police car. Destination?' '

Freda was indignant. 'That so-called destination was just an all-night chemist! They very kindly took me there *and brought me back*!'

'The newsboys thought you'd been arrested.'

'A little premature weren't they?'

'A little, perhaps, but . . . ' Howard smiled twistedly. ' . . . I think, *only a little*.'

Freda was about to make an angry retort at this insinuation when a voice sounded from the garden terrace outside.

'Mr. Nutting!'

Freda glanced in surprise towards the garden. 'It's old Cock Robin! What's he here again for?' She turned to her bedroom, still holding her unfinished coffee. 'Get rid of him, Howard! We had more than enough of him last night.'

'I don't think I can do that. It'll be *you* he wants to see.'

Freda stopped in her tracks, her lips tightening.

'Perhaps you ought to take off that gown, dear, and get dressed,' Howard murmured dryly. 'He may think that you're a loose woman.'

Freda glared at him for a moment, and then quickly disappeared into her bedroom.

'Mr. Nutting!' The inspector's voice sounded again from outside.

Howard opened the curtains and unbolted the garden door.

Inspector Robin stood outside, waiting to be admitted. 'May I come in this way?'

'Surely.' Howard motioned him inside. 'Morning, Inspector.'

'Morning, Mr. Nutting.' Robin looked around him. 'I've seen you *before* this morning, sir. At Mrs. Webb's.'

Howard nodded easily. 'I just called to see how the poor woman was. But your sergeant wasn't exactly a mine of information.'

Robin gave a tight smile. 'Understandable. She's vanished . . . without a word!'

'Good God!'

'We took her home last night, as you know,' Robin went on. 'Later, she phoned the station, and asked to see me again. We went there and took down a statement, and . . . ' He broke off at the sound of a bedroom door opening, and turned to see Freda emerging.

'Good morning, Mrs. Nutting.'

'Good morning, Inspector.'

'Did you get a good night's sleep?'

'*Too* good, thank you.'

Robin coughed uneasily. 'Then perhaps we could try to get a clearer picture of things. Couldn't really do much last night . . . Mrs. Webb and yourself being so upset.' The inspector pulled out some notes, giving them a quick glance before returning them to his pocket. 'Now, madam, about your burglar — '

Freda stared at him blankly for a second or two. 'Just what the hell do you mean, Inspector?' she exploded. '*My* burglar!'

Inspector Robin looked contrite. 'Perhaps I should have said *the* burglar. I'm sorry, Mrs. Nutting.'

'Oh, don't be!' Freda snapped. 'I know you think he's all my own work — that I'm making him up. Your sergeant as good as said so last night. Damned cheek!'

'Freda! Watch your tongue!' Howard warned her sharply.

Freda was unrepentant. ' 'Your burglar'! As if I'd *invented* him. As if he didn't *exist*!'

Robin tightened his lips. 'No need to fly off like that, madam. If he exists, we shall find proof of it.'

'I should have thought a dead body proof of it!' Freda retorted scornfully.

'The dead body is proof of the murderer . . . not the burglar,' Robin said quietly, unperturbed.

'It's the same thing!' Freda insisted. 'He got in to steal, didn't he? He was disturbed and had to kill to make his getaway.' She looked challengingly at the Inspector.

'Sound reasoning . . . ' he admitted.

'Thank you!'

' . . . but, I'm afraid, unsupported by evidence.' He looked at Freda's angry face. 'You say he got in here to steal. How, exactly?'

Freda remained silent.

'You thought last night he was a phoney television engineer,' Robin prompted gently.

'I only thought that because I had earlier telephoned for service.'

Robin shrugged. 'A call for service produces a genuine one, surely, not a phoney one?'

'Don't you read the papers, Inspector? The genuine one tips off a pal. Then they share the proceeds of the job. That's how they work it.'

Robin smiled grimly. 'There won't be any rush to share the proceeds of last night's job, I'm sure.'

Freda glared. 'Always cases like it in the papers.'

'Then I must keep my eyes open.'

Freda frowned, thinking. 'It doesn't have to be a phoney T.V. man, though, does it?'

'Not as far as I'm concerned,' Robin agreed.

'*Anybody* could have wandered in that side door,' Freda asserted.

Robin shook his head. 'Not at that time. The door is bolted.'

Freda was unwilling to forgo her new line 'The tenants go to the dustbins at all times. They unbolt it . . . '

The inspector dismissed the idea. 'That is absolutely forbidden.' He glanced at Howard. 'You, as tenants, know that.'

Howard nodded. 'Quite true.'

'There is some talk about it,' Freda agreed reluctantly.

'A very strict rule, the porter says,' Robin said. 'It was formulated as the result of a burglar getting in last year.'

'Proves we get burglars, doesn't it?' Freda pointed out.

'But it doesn't prove you got one last night.' Robin remained unimpressed.

Howard decided to get involved. He moderated the hitherto terse tone he had used to Freda, appearing to be helpful. 'You might have left the door unbolted when you emptied the paper bin, dear.'

'Good God, yes!' Freda seized on his words. 'Yes, that's when . . . '

Howard cut in: 'Oh, but you couldn't have.'

'Why?'

'Because you changed your mind and *didn't* empty it. I was using it . . . ' Howard smiled smugly. ' . . . remember?'

'Yes, dear.' Freda scowled.

'My men found the door securely bolted,' Robin asserted. 'And in any case, getting into the building doesn't get him into this flat, does it?'

'No, of course not,' Howard agreed readily.

The inspector regarded Freda steadily. 'You told us that you went out *before* your husband?'

'I did. I left here at six-thirty.'

'And where did you go?'

'The same place as I told your sergeant last night,' Freda said peevishly. 'A little theatre club in Bickmore Street.'

'Name?'

'The Five and Nine. There I met my friend Lucy, of touring days, and we had gin and memories.'

'Gin and . . . ?'

'Lucy's with lemon, mine with a cherry.'

'Freda!' Howard frowned.

'Don't interrupt me, Howard. The inspector wants all the details. He's getting them.'

'I'm very grateful, I'm sure,' Robin murmured.

Freda glanced triumphantly at Howard. 'You see?'

'How long did you stay at your club, madam?'

'Two hours. I left about quarter to nine, jumped in a cab, and came straight here. *And* the porter saw me come in.'

Robin nodded, making a note. 'And, having arrived, you came straight to the hall door here?'

'Naturally.'

'By way of the stairs?' Freda nodded. 'Did you see Mr. Webb anywhere?' Robin asked deliberately. 'Before you opened your door? Coming down the stairs? Or in the corridor?'

'No. I never saw him.'

Robin's busy eyebrows rose. 'Yet, within seconds of your opening the door, he was . . . there.'

'Within seconds?' Freda frowned.

'Before you had time to shut the door,' Robin said shrewdly. 'Or he couldn't have come in, could he? He had no key.'

Freda thought quickly. 'I didn't shut the door.'

Robin's expression betrayed his surprise. 'You had come in for the night. You were alone.'

'The room was stuffy from the central heating,' Freda countered. 'Always is. I like to get a bit of air moving.'

'I see.' Robin made another note. 'So . . . you came in. To about where?'

Freda moved to a point between the desk and the settee. 'Hereabouts.'

'What for?' Robin asked sharply.

'To . . . put my bag down on the desk.'

The inspector went up to the door and, as he spoke, demonstrated each of the points he wanted to make.

'So, instead of shutting the door, putting your handbag down here, and taking off your things . . . you left the door open, kept your street things on, and came straight to this point?'

'Yes.'

'What happened then?'

Freda became animated. 'A scarf was put over my head from behind, and a voice threatened to strangle me. I showed the scarf to your sergeant last night. It was in . . . ' She pointed to the rack at the hall door. ' . . . a pocket of my coat.'

Robin nodded. 'I have seen it. When . . . the voice . . . threatened to strangle you, what words were used?'

Freda scowled, and pointed to the notebook in the inspector's hand. 'You've got them there! What are you trying to do? Catch me out?'

'Freda!' Howard, who had been listening intently, spoke quietly. 'Stop being smart.'

'That's good advice your husband has just given you, madam,' Robin said. 'Now, what were the words the murderer used?'

"'Not one little dickey bird, or your face'll turn blue.'"

'What accent did the voice have?' Robin asked sharply.

'Accent?'

'Cockney? Irish? Northern, West Country? Public school? B.B.C.?' As Freda looked at him blankly, he added: 'An actress would notice such things.'

'When she's being strangled?' Freda was scornful. 'Besides, he didn't really speak, he just hissed in my ear. I never noticed any accent.'

Robin continued his interrogation. 'What age did he seem?'

'In his twenties, I'd say.'

'You said you caught only the barest glimpse of his face over your shoulder.'

Freda nodded. 'It seemed . . . blurred. I think he had a stocking mask on.'

'And you can't describe what he wore?'

'No! Because he had my head drawn back. All I could see was the ceiling.'

'What happened next?' Robin prompted.

'I screamed . . . blue murder!'

Bushy eyebrows rose again. 'In spite of

his warning not to cry out?'

'I'm a great believer in noise at such a time. It frightens them away. And it brings help.'

'Who did you think might come to *your* help?'

'Somebody! Anybody! With that scarf tightening on my windpipe, I wasn't going to be too fussy.'

'The porter?' Robin prompted. 'You knew he was there. You'd just spoken to him . . . And you had left this door open. He would be likely to hear anyone screaming blue murder . . . ' He paused, then added: 'Yet he heard no scream of any kind.'

Freda was unfazed. 'Then it was lucky Mr. Webb did, wasn't it?'

'For *you*, yes.' Robin changed his line of questioning abruptly. 'May I see your front-door key, please?'

Freda looked in her bag but could not find her key. 'That's funny. It's not here . . . '

The inspector was watching her closely. Howard was frowning thoughtfully.

'I had it last night,' Freda muttered. 'I

let myself in with it. I had it in my hand when he attacked me.'

'Are you sure?' Robin asked quietly. 'Or had you, earlier, given it to Mr. Webb?'

'No.'

'Mrs. Webb found a key to this door in her husband's overcoat.'

Freda was recovering her composure. 'That's possible,' she said easily. 'I lent him one some time ago.'

'Why?'

'He left some belongings here. Private papers. He might have wanted them when I was away.' She looked at Robin defiantly, waiting for his next attempt — so she imagined — to trip her up.

'If you'll humour me,' Robin said, 'I'm putting myself in the position of the strangler behind your door.' He went out. 'So . . . ' He opened the door. ' . . . before he set about strangling you . . . ' He kicked the door closed with his right foot. ' . . . the murderer didn't kick the door shut. One would have thought he'd appreciate privacy for such an operation. So Mr. Webb, who happened to be passing, heard your screaming and came to your rescue. Go on from there, please.'

'I knew he'd be no match for this young thug,' Freda said, 'so I shouted: 'Get Howard's gun!''

Robin frowned. 'Was that instruction sufficient? Did he know where it was kept?'

'No.' Freda shook her head. 'If he had known, he'd be alive now.' She went over and opened the secret cupboard in the bookcase, the door of which looked like the spines of half-a-dozen books.

'Then?' Robin prompted.

'The burglar realised he must find the gun first.'

'So?'

Freda resumed her story: 'He pushed me into my bedroom and shut the door.'

The inspector regarded her bedroom door. He pushed it open a little and glanced in. 'How long were you in here?'

'A matter of minutes, I suppose.'

'What did you do in here?'

'I listened, petrified. I heard them struggling, gasping! Then the gun went off . . . and I heard a body fall. Then . . . silence. Then . . . steps coming to the door. I threw myself on the bed and buried my face . . . certain that I was next . . . ' She paused, shuddering.

'Then?' Robin prompted again.

'I must have blacked out for a while. Next, I realised that all was quiet. I opened the door, and came out. There was no sign of him . . . But Mr. Webb was lying there . . . the gun nearby . . . I knelt over him and called his name. I realised he was dead. Suddenly there was knocking on the door. I opened it, and Mrs. Webb came in.'

'How did you know it was Mrs. Webb?' Robin asked sharply.

'I *didn't* know . . . not till later.'

'What did she do?'

'She took one look, and went raving mad! Tried to get the gun . . . to shoot me. Luckily, I was quicker than her. Not having seen the burglar, she thought *I'd* done it! I screamed at her that a burglar had killed her husband. I pushed her into that chair and called the police. Then I locked myself in my bedroom until you came.'

Robin paused in his rapid note-taking,

then: 'Did you open the garden window at all?'

'No.'

'My men found it open when they got here. Also the back gate.'

'Naturally. The burglar made off that way.'

Robin glanced at his earlier notes. 'The porter knew the dead man as Mr. Bliss. He'd let Flat Fourteen to him. You helped in the arrangements.'

'I merely mentioned that the flat was becoming empty.'

'Why,' Robin asked slowly, 'did Mr. Webb call himself 'Bliss'?'

'He didn't.'

'He took the flat in that name.'

'The flat *was* for a Mr. Bliss,' Freda explained, 'one of the agency's American executives.'

'The Sun Tan Travel Agency have no American connections, and no executive called Mr. Bliss,' Robin said heavily.

'That's what he *told* me.' Freda was unfazed. 'And that's what I told the porter.' She looked at him defiantly. 'That's all I know.'

'You know now that he wanted the flat for himself.'

'Yes.'

'And you know why?'

Freda nodded. 'Wife trouble. When he moved out of their marital home, he moved to his club at first. But a time limit operates there.'

Robin glanced upwards. 'When did he move in?'

'Two days ago.'

Robin gave her a frank look. 'Just how friendly were you, madam, with Mr. Webb?'

'We were just good friends,' Freda said quickly.

'Just *how* good?'

Freda spread her hands. 'Good enough to . . . try to help him . . . when he was depressed . . . with his wife's inhuman treatment.'

Robin looked up from his note-taking. 'Was that often?'

Howard, standing off to one side and staying out of the exchanges, was thinking that his wife was giving the greatest acting performance of her career. He smiled tightly, said nothing.

'Often enough, poor man. He'd phone, sometimes . . . upset as hell . . . desperate for someone to talk to . . . would I meet him for a drink?'

'And you'd meet him?' Robin asked sharply.

'Yes,' Freda admitted, shrugging. 'Only common humanity, wasn't it?'

Robin turned to a fresh page in his notebook, pencil poised. 'Where would you meet?'

'At a little pub near his office. I would listen to his troubles, and advise him as best I could.'

'Did you ever advise him to *leave* his wife?

Freda frowned angrily. 'Well, for God's sake!'

'Did you?' Robin was relentless.

'Certainly not.' Freda gave him a disdainful look. 'And if she told you that . . . '

'What advice did you give him?'

Freda reflected, then: 'I told him to sleep at his club for a night or two, to maybe frighten her. Remind her which side her bread was buttered. And who was buttering it . . . ' Her voice rose. 'But that was not advising him to leave her!'

There was a pause as Robin scribbled industriously. Then he looked up and turned to Howard.

'Mr. Nutting, you'd been away from home, you said?'

Howard nodded promptly. 'For two weeks, Inspector.'

Robin flicked back a couple of pages in his notebook. 'Returning here yesterday?'

'Correct.'

'So that it could not have been *your* electric razor which Mrs. Norman, your daily woman, came across in the bathroom three mornings ago?'

Howard merely smiled, and gave a 'search me' shrug.

Both men looked at Freda expectantly, waiting for her explanation.

'Mrs. Norman, for your information,' Freda said venomously, 'is my sworn enemy, because two days ago I sacked her for stealing. She begged me, in this very room, not to put the police on to her. Like a fool, I listened.'

Robin continued probing. 'The walls of these flats are quite thin. On that same morning, the people whose bedroom adjoins yours . . . heard a — ' He consulted his notes briefly. ' — 'rich baritone', singing 'Try a Little Tenderness'.'

'Probably someone on the radio,' Freda said briefly.

'Someone on the radio,' Robin said with heavy sarcasm, as he consulted his notes again, 'would hardly shout in the middle of it, 'Three rashers for me, sweetheart!''

'That's it!' Freda was indignant. 'Put the worst possible construction on a bit of human kindness! The night before these remarkable discoveries, Mr. Webb had phoned me. He was more depressed than I had ever known him to be before.'

'Over his wife?'

'Who else? He talked of suicide. He desperately wanted someone to talk to . . . '

Howard thought: 'A remarkable piece of acting . . . or is it *all* acting?'

'It was very late,' Freda went on. 'I had

already gone to bed. But I couldn't refuse him my help when he was in that state. I told him to come over . . . for a drink, and a talk. And to use my husband's bed for the night. Then he'd feel better in the morning.'

'His 'rich baritone' and healthy appetite seem to have proved you right,' Robin remarked, smiling faintly.

'It's a pity the neighbours don't mind their own business,' Freda snapped.

Robin made no apology. 'What neighbours do *is* neighbours' business . . . ' His next words, carefully spoken, caused Freda to give a little start. 'My man found a note here last night.'

'Note?' Freda said sharply. 'What note?'

The inspector produced the note and read from it.

' "Damn you! Stop pestering me. Thanks for the memory. Goodbye. Bernard." '

Freda frowned. 'You found that? Where?'

Robin pointed. 'On that settee over there.'

'Where Madam Webb put it!' Freda snapped. 'So let's have so nonsense about that!'

'Did you see her put it there?

'Course not.'

'She hid it among the cushions, do you mean?' Robin suggested.

'Obviously.'

'So that you couldn't find it?'

Fred snorted. 'So that *you could*.'

Robin raised his bushy eyebrows. 'I don't follow you.'

'For God's sake!' Freda was becoming exasperated at the inspector's relentless probing. 'She clearly put it there to incriminate me, didn't she? To make it seem I had a motive for murdering her husband.'

'But when did you last see the note?' Robin asked.

'See it?'

'Yes!' Robin's tone harshened. Howard wondered if he was about to lose his temper at what he perceived as Freda's apparent stupidity. 'Where was the note?' He looked round the flat. 'Where did Mrs. Webb get it from?'

Freda wrinkled her brow. 'From the postman, of course.'

'Are you seriously telling me that Mr. Webb sent this note to his wife and not to you?'

'Too true I am! Too true he sent it to her!' Freda's agitation was well-founded, since she herself had dictated the note to Bernard Webb for him to send to his wife. But, of course, she could not admit that to the inspector.

Robin showed her an envelope. 'This envelope bears *your* name and address . . . ' he began.

Freda cut him short with an angry gesture.

'*That's* the envelope your sergeant rummaged in my dustbin and found last night. It's got nothing to do with that note!'

Robin was not impressed. 'We've had a look at it. Same pen, ink, handwriting . . . '

Freda snorted impatiently. 'Yes, it's Mr. Webb's. He sent me a theatre ticket in that envelope. Piccadilly Theatre . . . night before last. I explained all this to your sergeant. I even showed him the programme to prove it.'

'I've seen it.' Robin was undeterred. 'He wasn't clear why Mr. Webb sent your ticket through the post.'

Freda sighed heavily. 'He had to see a man on that evening, which meant he wouldn't be able to get to the theatre with me for the start of the play. He didn't want my enjoyment to be spoiled.'

Robin's eyes narrowed. 'The theatre says that both tickets were presented together.' He referred to his notes, added: 'Dress Circle A9 and A10.'

'That's because he *was* able to get there for the start after all. The man cancelled the appointment.'

'What man?' Robin was like a dog with a bone.

'What man?' Freda threw up her hands. 'How would I know what man? His job was to see all kinds of people at all times. He didn't tell me about his appointments.'

'He told you about *this* one,' Robin persisted.

Freda glared at him in exasperation. 'Only because it affected our visit to the theatre. Oh, can't you *see*? His wife has destroyed the proper envelope and brought that note here to . . . '

Watching their verbal sparring from out of their line of sight, Howard was smiling quietly to himself in the background. He seemed to be enjoying Freda's discomfiture.

'To what?' Robin asked pointedly.

'To make it seem I killed her husband,' Freda said bitterly.

'How could that be? She didn't know he was dead until she got here.'

Howard smiled tightly. He was appreciating the inspector's doggedness and logic.

But Freda was holding to her line with equal determination. 'Her intention was to kill him and leave the note. But the burglar saved her the trouble.'

Robin seized on the apparent flaw. 'And how was she going to kill him? She could hardly know there was a loaded gun waiting . . . in a secret cupboard . . . in a room she had never entered

. . . and where she had to knock to gain admittance.'

The inspector looked again at the note.

''Thanks for the memory.'? Hardly the kind of note a husband would write. Much more like . . . a man ending an affair, don't you think?'

'The note is a note of dismissal . . . and hate! He didn't hate me . . . '

'No!' Robin said. 'But if he'd dismissed you, *you* might have hated *him*.'

Freda's self-control was slipping. Her protestations became almost frantic. 'He didn't . . . dismiss me! What's she been telling you?'

Robin played his next card. 'When you returned from your club, Mr. Webb was waiting for you . . . in his flat upstairs.'

'That's not true!' Freda protested hotly.

'And do you know who was waiting with him? His wife.'

'What lies . . . '

Robin glanced at his earlier notes. 'They had talked of their foolishness in quarrelling, and they had decided to forgive and forget and make a fresh start.'

164

Freda sneered. 'What pack of lies is this?'

'They were going home together,' Robin went on stolidly, looking up from his notes. 'But he insisted on one thing first. He must see you, explain things, and part as friends. He wanted to apologise for the harsh note he had sent you. To this, his wife consented.'

'God!' Freda scowled.

'He knew you would be back at nine,' Robin continued relentlessly, 'for it was to be with him that you were coming back.'

Freda clenched her fingers in frustration. 'She's invented . . . all of it . . . '

'From the window, he saw you get out of your cab. He left his wife and came down to you.' He paused, then: 'What happened in this room, we can only guess. But I think we can guess fairly accurately. He expected understanding. He met . . . blind rage.

'Upstairs, his wife waited, overjoyed that he was coming back to her. She heard a bang, but thought it was the traffic. It was only when her husband didn't return that it crossed her mind it could have been a gunshot . . . and that it could have been in the building . . . perhaps in the room below.'

'God! Such lies!' Freda was simmering.

Robin resumed his reconstruction. 'She hurried down. The door was shut. She banged on it, and you opened it. She found her husband dead, and no one with him but you.'

'She's lying!' Freda was almost choking with rage. 'She's lying about him coming back to her! And about my killing him! *And* about the note! It was sent to *her*, not to *me*! She's lying about everything! Oh, God! How wicked! How wicked!'

Freda finally subsided in tears.

'You'd better come along to the station, madam,' Robin said implacably. 'Give us a complete statement.'

'Yes.' Freda's voice was now a hushed whisper.

Robin turned to Howard. 'Would you get a coat, sir?'

Howard nodded and went to the clothes rack. 'What coat are you going to wear, dear,' he asked silkily, 'your black one?' He came over to her with the coat.

Mutely, she put it on as the inspector held the door open. Wearily, Freda picked up her bag and turned to the door.

But halfway there, she seemed to come to a sudden decision and stopped. She looked at Robin and sighed heavily. 'All right . . . I shall have to tell you the truth.'

To Howard's astonishment, she shrugged off her coat and threw it over the back of the settee. She sat down defiantly.

The inspector closed the door and moved nearer to her.

Howard watched the tableau intently, alert and amused.

Robin broke the long silence. 'And the truth is . . . there was no burglar?' he prompted.

Freda smiled grimly. 'There *was* a burglar, all right. He came . . . by invitation.'

'Invitation? Whose?' Robin's eyebrows betrayed his surprise.

'Mr. Webb's.'

'For what purpose?'

'To murder my husband.' Freda sat

back, throwing a triumphant glance at her husband. Howard remained expression-less.

'Webb brought a man here to murder your husband?' Robin asked, incredulous. 'How can *you* know this?'

'I know all right.'

'Then you knew last night?'

'Yes.'

Robin frowned. 'Why didn't you tell us?'

Freda hesitated, giving the impression that she was having an inner struggle with herself. 'I wouldn't blacken the name of a dead man . . . and a dear friend.'

This 'revelation' brought a definite reaction from Howard. He opened his mouth to speak, then thought better of it as the inspector rapped out a further question:

'Why are you telling me now?'

Freda spread her hands. 'To defend myself against that lying woman, of course. What else can I do?' She looked at Robin beseechingly. He opened his notebook again.

'Right! Then let's *have* the truth.'

Freda took a deep breath, then: 'Webb was obsessed with the idea of murdering my husband. Kept coming to me with plots and ideas. He even wanted me to help him!'

'Didn't you think it your duty to warn your husband, or tell us?' Robin demanded sharply.

Freda shrugged. 'You don't suppose I took the man seriously, do you? I just laughed at him ... ' Her voice and expression changed as she became tearful again. 'I see *now* he was serious. It's all ended in tragedy ... ' She dabbed at her eyes with a handkerchief. 'In a way, I'm glad he's ... gone.'

'Why?' Robin demanded briefly.

'He was ill. Ambitious, but not getting anywhere, stuck in that dismal travel agency all day ... the frustration of it was ... altering his whole personality, making him bitter. He wanted to be free ... to create ... '

'Yes, yes.' Robin waved a hand impatiently, stopping her flow of words. 'Mrs. Nutting, tell me all you know about last night's affair.'

'Webb arranged for Vic to come here . . . '

'Vic?' Robin interrupted sharply. 'Was that the burglar's name?'

'Yes.' Freda bit her lip, regretting her slip in revealing the name.

'You say Webb 'arranged' things,' Robin said thoughtfully. 'Bribed him, do you mean?'

Freda nodded. 'Part bribery, part blackmail. He promised him four hundred pounds.'

Robin looked up from scribbling in his notebook. 'How was he able to blackmail him?'

'He said Vic had a criminal record, but was now working in a position of trust somewhere.'

'Did he say where?'

'No.'

'What was Vic to do? Did he tell you?'

Freda nodded. 'He was to turn up here as the T.V. man.'

Robin gave a little grunt, as he mentally moved a piece in this confused jigsaw. 'So that's where you got *him* from?'

'Where else?' Freda regarded him calmly.

'And how was the murder to be done? Did he say?'

Freda nodded. 'He was to do it as soon as he was let in. With that ornament over there.' She pointed. 'Webb would return and give him the four hundred. He would also take the Bingo money. So that the boys would be blamed for everything.'

'Where would you be while all this was going on?' Robin asked.

'At my club. Webb knew it was my evening out. That's obviously why he chose last night.'

Robin looked up from his notebook. 'To give you an alibi, do you mean?'

Freda frowned. 'Certainly not. He couldn't *do* it if I was *here*, could he?'

'How would the boys get the blame for it?'

'Only they knew the Bingo money was here,' Freda said quickly. 'It would be assumed they came to steal it, were disturbed by my husband, and they had to . . . silence him. Webb would help the story along by saying he'd seen two boys

171

hanging round the back gate earlier.'

Howard, who had been listening in increasing agitation, suddenly boiled over:

'Well, of all the . . . '

Robin checked him. 'Just a minute, sir!' He turned to Freda. 'Have you any idea why Vic didn't . . . carry out his contract? With so much to gain?'

Freda spread her hands. 'He'd have more to gain by getting rid of his blackmailer. And he'd get the Bingo money just the same. Two birds, one stone.'

'He slipped up there,' Robin said dryly, 'because your husband put it in the safe.'

'Yes. We know that now.'

'But he got the four hundred that Webb brought with him?'

Freda shrugged. 'I don't see it anywhere.' Her tone was sarcastic.

Howard could hold back no longer. 'What a load of old rubbish!'

Robin's eyebrows rose as he turned to regard him. 'Eh?'

'The very idea!' Howard said scathingly. 'My boys coming up here to pinch my money and murder me! If they wanted the Bingo money, why not pinch it down there in comfort?'

'Could they have?' Robin asked keenly.

'I don't see why not. They had charge of it overnight.' Howard paused, then added tellingly: 'They *guard* it for me, Inspector.'

'I see.' Robin completed a hasty note. 'But did Webb know that?'

'My wife did!' Howard remarked sardonically. He watched the effect of his words had on Freda, considerably amused. 'When he brought his murder plots to her, she would surely point out any little . . . snags . . . in them.'

Freda recovered herself quickly.

'Which, of course I did. He maintained the boys would not . . . foul their own doorstep.'

Howard was not yet finished. 'The murder planned for me wasn't a shoddy little fake burglary job!' he said deliberately, looking at the inspector. 'It was imaginative! Sophisticated!'

'Oh? What makes you think so?'

'Certain little discoveries I've made, Inspector,' Howard said smugly.

'Such as?' Robin was interested.

Howard went and retrieved the drawer from his bedroom, and showed the items in it to the Inspector. 'Artistic photography ... ' he remarked sarcastically, showing Robin the pictures. The inspector was puzzled by one of them. 'I think it goes the other way up,' Howard said helpfully. The inspector turned the picture round. 'It's the all-in wrestling influence.'

Howard glanced at Freda, who sat grimacing slightly. He was enjoying her discomfort.

The inspector put aside the pictures and looked briefly at the other items in the drawer.

'Also,' Howard went on, pointing, 'cotton-wool in my keyhole; my bolt, which I never use — ' He operated it. ' — oiled, and made to work.'

The inspector checked the items carefully, frowning thoughtfully. 'How did you come to discover all this, Mr. Nutting?'

'Last night,' Howard spoke casually, 'I tried to look through my keyhole to see what your men were up to. I found hair oil on my nose. It had run down the door. When I came to pack ... for the Berrington ... the key of my drawer was missing. I found it in the sideboard.'

'Just what does all this add up to?' Robin asked pointedly.

Freda, who been sitting silently on the settee, grim and worried, suddenly spoke up. 'No need to create such a mystery, Howard.'

He gave her an amused glance. 'I'm not creating one, dear. I'm reporting one.'

Robin regarded Freda sternly. 'Mrs. Nutting, have you ... ?'

'I said I'd tell you everything, Inspector,' Freda snapped, with a hateful glare at her husband. 'But I don't see how I can if I'm not allowed to. If I am constantly interrupted ... '

Robin coughed politely. 'Please carry on, Mrs. Nutting.'

'Vic refused the Fake Burglary job, so Outrageous Suggestion was decided on.'

'Outrageous Suggestion?' Robin asked, puzzled.

'Yes. In it, my husband is murdered by

a young man he brings home and tries to seduce. It was Vic's idea.'

'Oh, no!' Howard exclaimed loudly, moving forward towards Freda.

'Please, sir!' Robin stepped between them. He indicated the drawer. 'What about this stuff?'

'Evidence of my sexual Jekyll-and-Hydery, Inspector. The whole idea comes from *my* notebook. Pinched by Webb.' Howard reached out his notebook, a foolscap-size lever-arch file, very old, and bursting at the seams.

'He hasn't been *near* your notebook,' Freda said sourly

Howard ignored her, and took out a newspaper cutting and an index card.

'There you are. 'Outrageous Suggestion'. The Leonard Black case. To murder me, Webb was going to reconstruct this eight-year-old crime.'

'May I see that?' Robin asked sharply, reaching for the cutting and examining it intently.

Howard read from the index card in his hand: ''Innocent boy clobbers elderly male seducer. Tried, acquitted.' Webb meant my murder to be a reproduction of that . . . *on the surface*.'

The inspector was smiling rather strangely as he looked at the cutting.

Howard went on, indicating the 'evidence' in the drawer: 'And these charming items — ' He glanced at Freda. ' — from my wife's wardrobe would scream my epitaph . . . 'Seducer of boys'! Deny it, who will? My youth work, Inspector, makes me a ready-made victim.'

Robin held up the cutting. 'Why do you keep this?' he asked, curiously.

'I write plays,' Howard said, indicating the notebook. 'Perfect little murder, don't you think?'

Robin frowned, muttered: 'I've thought so for eight years . . . ' He seemed to almost be talking to himself. Then he turned to Freda. 'You're certain Webb said it was Vic who thought things up?'

'Quite certain.'

The buzzer sounded, and Howard crossed to answer it.

'Nutting . . . Yes, hang on . . . ' He turned to the inspector. 'For you. It's your sergeant.'

The inspector took over at the instrument. 'Inspector Robin . . . Who . . . ? Can't he give it to you . . . ? All right, I'm coming down. I'll want the car to go to the station.' He replaced the buzzer, and carefully laid the cutting on the desk. Then he headed for the door. 'Excuse me, I'll be back in a moment.'

After he had went out through the hall door, closing it behind him, there was a long silence. Freda sat smoking. Her face was a mask.

Howard regarded her amusedly, shaking his head and making little tutting noises. 'Very serious, Mrs. Nutting . . . lying to the police.'

'As Madam Webb will find out before long!' Freda snapped.

Howard wandered over to his desk and looked at the cutting again. 'Good God!' he breathed.

'What?'

'I *thought* the inspector was getting a bit excited about this,' Howard said, holding up the cutting. 'This was one of his cases!'

Freda tightened her lips, but said

nothing. She rose to hang her black coat back on the rack.

Howard turned from putting his file away. 'Better leave it handy. You're going to need it.'

Freda ignored him, and hung the coat on the rack. 'If you're living at the Berrington now, why don't you go there?'

'What?' Howard laughed shortly. 'And miss all the fun? Miss seeing you and the inspector go out of that door, hand-in-handcuff?'

'It's Madam George Washington Webb who will be doing that,' she said venomously. 'She won't get away with her damned lies.'

Howard raised his eyebrows. '*Her* lies? Why don't you sit down before you drop dead?'

'The lies *I* told last night,' Freda said defensively, 'I told to shield *her* husband . . . '

'Whose husband?'

' . . . because I wouldn't blacken the name of a dead man,' Freda finished piously.

Howard mocked her by miming sad

violin music whilst she was talking.

'But now I see what her game is,' Freda said decisively. 'I shall tell everything I know . . . no more lies.'

The doorbell rang, and Howard opened the door. Inspector Robin came briskly into the room. In his hand was a letter which he had obviously just opened. Apparently, he intended on going out again shortly, because he left the door open.

'Mrs. Nutting! Good news for you! Mrs. Webb's solicitor's just brought this . . . ' He waved the letter, as Freda looked at him in astonishment. 'Signed by her. A couple of hours ago. She admits she lied.'

'About that note?' Freda asked sharply.

Robin nodded. 'And about the reconciliation upstairs with her husband. It never took place.'

Freda regarded both men in triumph. 'You *see*?'

Robin glanced at the letter. 'She lied . . . to make you suffer. Perfectly understandable, I suppose.'

'Huh!' Freda gave a snort.

'So that's why she's run off,' Robin explained. 'Frightened of what she's done ... ' He turned back to the doorway. 'Excuse me. I'll be back in a second.' He looked at Freda before going out. 'I thought you ought to know straight away.'

'Thank you, Inspector.'

Resuming his journey to the door Robin paused, and added over his shoulder: 'I hope Mrs. Webb doesn't do anything foolish.'

6

As the door closed, Freda looked curiously at Howard. 'What does he mean?'

Her husband glared at her, tight-lipped and very angry. 'He means she might kill herself.'

Freda seated herself on the settee. 'Kill herself? Why should she?'

'If she thinks she'll be accused of the murder,' Howard fretted.

'She won't be accused now that I've told the truth about Vic,' Freda pointed out.

'Janet doesn't *know* that!' Howard snapped. 'She still thinks the inspector believes that either you or she killed Webb. And that if *you* aren't accused, *she* will be.'

'Nonsense!' Freda scoffed. 'She can't think that, or she wouldn't have confessed.'

'You wouldn't understand *her* motives,' Howard said, biting out the words with hatred of his wife. 'Some people are *human*, Freda. Janet Webb happens to be such a one.'

'Indeed?' Freda sneered. 'I thought telling all those filthy lies so that I would rot in prison for years was just a tiny bit *in*human. Of course, I may be unusually sensitive.'

'Don't worry. You're not. Janet reacted perfectly naturally. She was hurt, so she hurt back.'

'You seem quite an authority on the woman.' Freda looked at him, smiling sardonically. 'Rather remarkable, isn't it, considering you'd never set eyes on her until last night? At least, that's what I'm expected to believe.'

'I met her for the first time last night,' Howard said stolidly.

'You'd met her before last night, Howard.' Freda's eyes were gleaming. 'I could tell . . . when she came out of that room . . . the way your eyes met. I wasn't born yesterday, you know!'

'No! But you *were* born!' Howard's voice rose to a shout. 'That's what's so bloody awful!'

'I've heard that before,' Freda snapped back. 'It's from one of your plays!'

The developing row was cut short when the doorbell rang again. Howard opened the door to admit the returning Inspector Robin. His expression showed that he was very obviously quietly excited about something.

'Well, we've got a line on that boy,' he announced. 'Works at some ice-cream factory, apparently. And not far away, either.'

Howard wrinkled his brow. 'Boy? What boy?'

Robin smiled. 'Of course, he'll be a man now. I keep forgetting.'

'You mean Leonard Black?' Comprehension dawned on Howard. The inspector was referring to the old case in the newspaper cutting.

'We're getting some prints from his locker. To check with those found here . . . ' Robin broke off as the buzzer sounded. 'I think that may be the car. May I?'

At Howard's nod, he went over to the buzzer.

'Robin here . . . Is the car back . . . ? Never mind his picture. We won't need that if we've got him. I want somebody to go to where he works . . . Mac? . . . Good, but I want a word with him first. Hold him a moment.' He hung up, and turned to Freda. 'With a bit of luck, we'll have him here for you to identify.'

As Robin hurried out again, he looked at Howard from the doorway. 'It would be something if we got him after eight years.'

Howard stood staring at the closed door, frowning in puzzlement.

'Well, we are learning about police methods.' Freda was grimly amused. 'Man with a Mission is Old Cock Robin. North West Mounty stuff. Always gets his man.'

'What?' Howard was abstracted.

'Looking for eight years, he has been . . . for a murder to hang on this Leonard man. And he's settled for ours.' Freda smiled grimly. 'Very flattering.'

'You're raving!' Howard protested. 'He can't pin Webb's murder onto Leonard Black.'

'Why not?' Freda demanded.

Howard pointed to the sideboard. 'Because the fingerprints found here on the Coca-Cola glass cannot be Leonard Black's, now, can they?'

'Only if the inspector says they are, dear,' Freda said smugly. 'He's bringing Leonard for me to identify as Vic. Even though he knows I never properly saw Vic.'

'Then you mustn't do it.'

Freda shrugged. 'I shall do what the Inspector wants. It'll be *best for me*, I'm sure.'

'But . . . '

'I'm sorry for Leonard, naturally,' Freda mused. 'But he'll only be getting what's due to him. He shouldn't have gone around murdering in the first place.'

'We don't even know that he *is* a murderer.' Howard was still dubious.

'The inspector doesn't appear in much doubt.'

'Leonard didn't murder Bernard Webb!' Howard was almost shouting again.

'Leonard will do!' Freda yelled, pointing to the door. 'Whoever the inspector brings will do! I don't care if it's a Chelsea Pensioner.'

'It could mean years of imprisonment for him!' Howard was appalled.

Freda shrugged. 'He owes them eight. So he's not doing so badly.'

Howard tightened his lips and took a step towards her. 'There will be no false identification while I'm around!' he warned.

Freda looked at him defiantly. 'I don't see how you can stop it. You never saw the murderer — '

Howard approached her, ugly and menacing. He grabbed hold of her hair brutally from behind, forcing her head back.

Freda was too startled to scream.

'I not only saw him,' Howard said gratingly, 'we got friendly. Had drinks. And he told me . . . the lot!' He jerked her head back painfully. 'Why don't I murder you now? It would give me so much *pleasure*!'

Now really frightened, Freda stared at him mutely.

'Webb wasn't the plotter,' Howard

stated flatly. 'He was only the backer. The Outrageous Suggestion idea was *yours*! All *yours*!'

'No, no!' Freda babbled. 'Vic thought of it. It was Vic's idea!'

Howard swung his hand, and slapped her face soundly. 'You said,' he gritted, 'no more lies. Remember?' He jerked her hair savagely.

'I swear to you it was Vic!' Freda gasped. 'I should never have . . . ohh!' She broke off as Howard slapped her again.

'No more lies. Remember?'

Freda gave a convulsive shudder, then slumped submissively. She realised she had to drop her pretence. Howard snarled: 'He so believed all that filth, he would have murdered me for nothing.'

'You think so?' Freda faltered.

Howard grabbed her by her shoulders, forcing his wife to look at him. 'But when he knew the truth, he asked to murder you. *Begged* to, to atone for his lunacy in believing you. And much as I would have loved to do it, I engaged him to . . . ' He paused, breathing hard. 'That's why he was behind the door. But Lover Boy poked his nose in. Lucky for you he did.'

Savagely, he slapped Freda again. She began whimpering.

'Oh, yes, your T.V. man came all right. I let him in . . . If Janet hadn't called from the bedroom . . . ' With a snarl, he threw her from him and went over to his desk.

'So she was here,' Freda muttered. 'I *knew* it.'

Howard nodded, smiling grimly. 'And she met Vic, too. She can stop any false identification.'

'What was she doing here?'

'Jumping into bed with me, of course,' Howard sneered.

'I see now,' Freda whispered. 'You planned it together . . . her lies and your silence to put me in prison.'

'Best place for you . . . '

'But her conscience has let you down.'

Howard ignored the remark. 'And when the inspector gets back, I'm doing all I can to put you in prison where you belong!'

Freda was recovering her courage. 'Go too fast and you'll put yourself there. And her as well. For withholding evidence

. . . diverting the course of justice.' Howard was silent, thinking. 'Engaged Vic to murder me, did you?' Freda went on. 'That makes us quits, anyhow.' She smiled slowly as she realised the implication of Howard's admissions. 'I'm sure the inspector would love to know all you've just told me. Your sympathy for this Leonard man has weakened your position considerably . . . ' She paused. Howard remained silent.

'If I were you, Howard, I should forget all about Leonard, and go along with the inspector and me.'

Still Howard remained silent. He was thinking furiously.

'Face the facts, dear. Vic has let us both down, hasn't he? We shan't see him again in a hurry. We've got to *have* a murderer. I'm no longer in the running . . . So it's either Leonard . . . or . . . Janet.'

Howard was suddenly roused. 'Janet?'

'Too bloody true, Janet!' Freda said venomously. 'Who had more motive? Nobody saw the shooting. Janet was around. She had a key to the door.'

'She found that *after* the murder.'

'Her story!' Freda was scornful. 'The story of a self-confessed liar. Why run away if she's innocent?'

'She's frightened.'

'She *should* be, too.' Freda saw the worry and indecision etched on Howard's face. 'He'll be coming back. Make up your mind,' she urged. 'Settle for Leonard. He *is* a murderer. He'll only be getting his just deserts. Plus eight years' freedom.' She paused, went on insinuatingly: 'Let Old Cock Robin get his man, and he'll soon forget what we've been up to. This eight-year dream obviously means a great deal to him. He could turn very nasty if you spoil everything.'

Howard considered her words painfully, then: 'No! *No!* And I speak for Janet as well!' He turned as the doorbell rang again.

He opened the door, admitting the inspector. 'That hall's busy,' he told Howard. 'I told them to put my calls up here. I hope you don't mind.'

'Carry on, Inspector.' Howard bit his lip, then said slowly: 'Inspector, my wife has something to tell you. And so have I — '

The telephone rang.

Robin looked quickly at Howard. 'May I?' At his nod, he strode to the instrument.

'Robin here . . . Yes, Mac . . . Yes . . . I'll be here.' He hung up. He appeared not to have heard Howard's last words. He wandered about the room, his manner urgent yet subdued.

Howard and Freda exchanged blank looks.

'Leonard's . . . bought a paper,' Robin said at last.

'Reading all about his murder?' Freda asked, frowning.

'He picked out some gee-gees. Then he put on a bet.'

'Thinks it's his lucky day,' Freda commented cynically.

'Leonard has had eight years of lucky days.' Robin smiled grimly.

Howard did not speak. He was now sick with indecision.

'Leonard's crime was . . . unbelievable,' Robin went on, pacing slowly about the room. 'That's how he got away with it . . . He was only fifteen. But he beat us all. Beat the hangman, too . . . with his birth certificate.'

Howard was now looking as though he would interrupt the Inspector any second. Freda was watching him in alarm.

'What he did . . . affected me . . . very personally.' Robin stopped his pacing and stood facing Freda and Howard. 'The man he murdered, Sir Felix D'Alton, was a brilliant surgeon. My wife owes her life to him. Me, my happiness. But for Sir Felix, I should go home to an empty house every night . . . He lessened this world's suffering. Yet *he* suffered unspeakably, at Leonard's hands.'

Howard was now making no attempt to interrupt. He stood fascinated by Robin's revelations.

'You see, he didn't kill him,' the inspector went on. 'Just injured him horribly, and ran out . . . When they found Sir Felix, three days later, he had been dead but a few hours. What he suffered is . . . unthinkable. The room . . . was a shambles . . . where he'd dragged himself . . . round and round . . . dying . . . insane at times . . . trying to reach the door, or the phone . . . '

Freda brought a hand to her mouth, horrified.

'Leonard dutifully came forward. Said Sir Felix inveigled him to the flat . . . tried to kiss him . . . He knew he couldn't be hanged. He was tried, acquitted; and, as you know, the public made a hero of the boy . . . The Innocent in the Wicked City . . . who would murder for his manhood.' Robin's voice was tinged with bitterness.

'The papers fought with their cheque-books for his story. I can see the headline now: 'I Struck for English Manhood' by Leonard Black. Which pleased Leonard no end. For he fancied himself as a writer. They paid him a thousand pounds. It all worked out as he had planned.

'You mean . . . ?' Howard found his voice.

'We learned later from his ex-girlfriend that he had his story all written *before* the murder.'

'Just waiting for a victim, do you mean?' Howard said slowly, beginning to see where Robin's words were leading.

Robin nodded sombrely. 'He took a job as a waiter at Sir Felix's Club.'

'But what *was* he doing in Sir Felix's flat?' Freda asked.

'Collecting a left-off suit which Sir Felix was giving him.'

'And . . . was Sir Felix . . . ?'

Robin tightened his lips. 'Only Leonard's word for it to this day. He was kind and cultured, a bachelor, living alone. Fertile soil for Leonard's invented story . . . Leonard's plan was a big success. We all try to repeat our successes in some way. For eight years I've prayed that Leonard Black would be no exception — ' He whirled around as the telephone rang again, snatched up the instrument.

'Robin here . . . Yes, Mac . . . Yes . . . That's the least of our worries . . . See what the prints say first . . . Then come here . . . ' The Inspector hung up, more than a little excited at the news he had just received.

'Leonard went from the betting shop to a public convenience. Mac followed.

Leonard went into a cubicle, Mac into an adjoining one. He spied at Leonard over the screen.'

'What was Leonard doing?' Howard asked dubiously. 'I mean . . . ?'

'Mac says he was eagerly reading about the murder,' Robin told him. 'Then he left in a hurry. Mac had trouble with the door and lost him. But they've got some prints and they're looking at them now.'

Howard volunteered some information that he considered pertinent. 'Inspector, the fingerprints on that glass are not Leonard's.'

'What glass?' Robin raised his bushy eyebrows.

'The Coca-Cola glass.'

Robin laughed shortly. '*That* glass? It was useless. Thousands of prints all over it. Might have come from a café.'

'But you said you found fingerprints here.' Howard frowned.

'So we did. A very nice set.' Robin smiled thinly. 'But not on a glass.'

'Then where?'

'On the underside of your water closet

seat. Mrs. Nutting was certain she left the seat and cover down. You didn't use it, yet we found the seat up.'

Howard and Freda exchanged startled glances.

'The murderer,' Robin went on, 'whilst waiting for his victim, would naturally be nervous. Suppose, to give himself courage, he'd had a couple of beers? Before long he'd have to obey a call of nature. He'd be unable to manage with his gloves on . . . '

He pointed to the bathroom.

'So, on his way there, he whipped them off. Found the seat down, so he lifted it.' He smiled thinly. 'We are dealing with a gentlemen, obviously.'

Freda and Howard remained silent, stunned and subdued.

The inspector waited, gazing thoughtfully at the telephone.

Suddenly the chimes of an ice-cream float sounded in the distance outside.

Howard heard them and looked across at Freda, who was showing growing disquiet. The inspector gave no sign that he had heard the chimes.

The chimes were heard again, a little nearer.

Howard looked at the inspector. 'Did you say Leonard worked in ice-cream?'

'Yes.'

'What does he do in ice-cream?' Howard asked tensely.

Robin looked at him. 'Makes it, I suppose.'

The chimes sounded again, this time a little nearer.

The inspector looked up sharply.

'He doesn't *sell* it, does he?' Howard jerked out.

Robin gave a start. 'Good God!'

The chimes sounded again, a little nearer.

'It's in the street, isn't it?' Howard said, going to the window to move aside the curtain and look out.

'Don't touch that curtain!' Robin warned him sharply. Howard stopped dead, watched the inspector crossing quickly to the hall door. 'Put out that light!'

Howard followed Robin's instruction, and switched off the main lighting. No bulb was glowing now, but sufficient light filtered in from the bright day outside for those inside to see what was going on. There was, however, deep shadow about the hall door.

'I must warn them,' Robin said, hurrying out of the room and leaving the door open.

Howard looked at his wife. 'He thinks it's Leonard.'

Freda tried to disguise the fear she was feeling. 'Stupid! Ice-cream men are on the on the streets every day — ' She broke off as the inspector came hurrying back into the room, this time shutting the door behind him.

'It could be him . . . scouting . . . to make sure the flat is empty!'

Howard frowned. 'Why?'

The chimes sounded again, apparently now receding.

Freda let out a sigh of relief. 'Gone away! Nothing to do with us.'

Tensely, they listened to the receding chimes.

The inspector, disappointed, risked a sly peep out of the window.

'We know murderers return to the scene,' Freda remarked crassly. 'But evidently not while the police are there.'

The inspector came away from the window, and shook his head at Freda. 'He doesn't know I'm here.'

'He doesn't know you're here, either, Freda,' Howard pointed out. 'The papers said you'd gone to Holloway.'

'And that you, sir, had moved into the Berrington.' Robin tightened his lips. 'If he's read that . . . ' The chimes sounded again — nearer this time. 'He's coming back! He wants to get in here!'

'What for?' Howard was puzzled.

Robin was becoming increasingly animated. 'I saw morning papers!' He darted a glance about him. 'Where are they, Mr. Nutting?'

The two men looked about for the papers, but in the gloom they could not find them.

'Put that desk light on,' Robin whispered. Howard did so, enabling them to find the papers. Freda was sitting like a stone, watching them. 'It's something he saw in that paper,' Robin muttered.

They started to scan the papers.

'Which paper did he have?' Howard asked.

'God knows. Mac didn't say.'

The chimes sounded again, now very near. 'He's just outside,' Howard said, moving towards his desk.

The inspector suddenly pointed to the desk light. 'It's shining on the curtain! Put it out!' Howard put out the desk light. 'Now I can't see a damn thing,' the policeman muttered irritably.

'For God's sake!' Howard protested. 'You just said . . . '

'The floor!' Robin snapped. 'Bring the light down to the floor!'

Howard brought the desk light to the floor and switched it on. By its light, both men, now on their knees, frantically searched the papers.

'It's something he read in that cubicle,' Robin muttered. 'Something he didn't know till then . . . '

Howard gave an exclamation, pointed to a passage in the newspaper he was examining. 'There! What my wife said!'

'What did she say?' Robin said briefly. 'Quickly!'

Robin read out the passage he'd spotted. ''Webb had a large sum of money on him. The police found none' . . . ' He looked up excitedly. 'He's coming for the money. He thinks it's still here!'

The buzzer suddenly sounded. The inspector scrambled up and went to the instrument.

'Yes . . . ? O.K . . . ' He hung up, and looked at Freda and Howard. 'He's in the building. Got in the side door.'

Robin hurried quickly into the hall, talked briefly to the policeman there, and returned, shutting the door. 'Hide, both of you. Switch off the light, Mr. Nutting.'

'But how can he get in here?' Howard looked at Robin, puzzled.

'Didn't your wife lose her key?'

The inspector picked up the newspaper from the floor, and wafted it to disperse Freda's cigarette smoke. 'Damned cigarette smoke everywhere!' he muttered.

Freda got up, looking very worried, and her eye caught Howard's. He was smiling as he put out the desk light, replacing it on the desk.

Freda went into her bedroom, whilst Howard went into his. Neither of them quite closed the doors.

The inspector threw the newspaper down on the desk, and went behind the floor-length curtains over the window behind the sideboard.

Seconds passed in utter silence.

Then the hall door slowly opened and a shadowy figure came quietly and furtively in, shutting the door.

The main lighting was switched on.

Janet, looking very frightened, was revealed standing at the switch. She looked round the room apprehensively.

Howard came hurrying out of his bedroom. 'Janet!'

He went over to her quickly, and held her to him.

'I can't face it!' Janet moaned. 'I can't! The police are looking for me. They think I did it. Oh! I'm so unhappy. I'm going to kill myself.'

The inspector stepped out from behind the curtains. Freda's wicked face appeared round her door.

'Later! Later!' Robin hissed. 'Hide, both of you!'

Howard whisked Janet into his bedroom, catching Freda's eyes as he did so. Her head withdrew back behind her door.

Robin wrinkled his nose. 'Now the place reeks of scent!' he muttered, picking up the the newspaper and doing his wafting act again. He threw the paper back on the desk, and was returning to his hiding place when he realised that the light was still on.

Muttering in exasperation, he put out the light and blundered back behind the curtain.

A minute later, the hall door slowly opened again, and a figure came cautiously in, quietly closing the door.

The main lighting snapped on.

Vic, in the garb of an ice-cream salesman, was at the switch. He looks round the room suspiciously, then hurried across to the desk and began to search frantically: first the pigeonholes, then the drawers.

He pulled out a drawer, placing it on

the top of the desk, and was searching in it when he suddenly stopped dead, seeing the morning paper lying there.

He grabbed it and looked at it, frowning. Alarmed and suspicious, he turned and looked quickly at the door.

The inspector stepped out and revealed himself, and the two men stood facing each other for a few seconds.

'Inspector Robin!' Vic gasped. 'Fancy meeting you!'

Robin stared at him impassively. 'Leonard Black! How you've grown! You're a man now.' He moved nearer to him. 'What are you looking for . . . ? The four hundred pounds?'

He reached for the morning paper, which was sticking out of Leonard Black's pocket. He waved it gently. 'It says here that you've got it.'

'I've never set eyes on it!' Black snapped. An expression of dawning comprehension crossed his face. He pointed to the paper. 'It's a trick! *She* said that to get me here.'

'She?' Robin prompted.

'That cow you took to Holloway.'

Freda stepped out from her bedroom. 'Somebody referring to me?' she said, sweetly.

Black started violently on seeing her. He was deeply shaken. 'What are you doing . . . out?'

'I was never *in*!' Freda grinned savagely.

'You're not pinning this on me!' Black snarled, turning to the Inspector. '*She* murdered him, Inspector! I was halfway down the garden when — '

'Liar!' Freda hissed.

Black spun towards the door, evidently thinking of making a dash for freedom.

Inspector Robin stopped him in his tracks. 'You wouldn't get far, sonny, and you might get hurt.'

Black thought better of it, and stood, breathing heavily.

Howard and Janet came out of the bedroom. Black saw them but gave no sign of recognition.

Robin looked at Freda. 'You said he took the money. It wasn't true?'

Thinking quickly, Freda pointed to the paper. 'I just said that to get him here.'

She smiled triumphantly. 'To prove to you that he existed.'

'She's just heard me say that!' Black snapped. 'Lying bitch!'

'That's enough of that,' Robin warned. Then, to Freda: 'Where *is* the four hundred?'

Freda laughed carelessly. 'Nowhere! Doesn't exist! Never did.' She looked distastefully at Leonard Black, a.k.a. 'Vic'. 'Just as well . . . with him around.'

The inspector moved over to where Janet and Howard were standing. 'Where have you been hiding?' he asked Janet.

'Upstairs.'

Robin smiled, not unkindly. 'You'll change your mind . . . about killing yourself.'

Howard put a protecting arm about her.

'Yes,' she whispered.

The inspector now contemplated Black. 'How's the writing going, Leonard? Still keen?'

He indicated his smock. 'Don't get much time for it on this job.'

Robin smiled grimly. 'Must do something about that . . . Suppose you come and make a nice long statement, eh?'

The inspector moved towards the hall door. While the policeman's back was turned, Black gave a thumbs-up sign to Howard and Janet. They smiled wanly back at him. He then gave Freda a long, withering look. 'Cow!' he hissed.

'Charming. Can't take you anywhere.' Freda smiled at him poisonously. 'Except that you're not *going* anywhere, are you?'

'When I've written my statement, *you* won't be going anywhere either.' Black glared at her hatefully.

The inspector held the door open, waiting for Black.

'Write your life story while you're at it,' Freda jeered at him. 'Call it, 'Sir Felix Rides Again'.'

At the mention of Sir Felix, a new fear grew in Black's face. He glanced sickly at the inspector but, finding his face expressionless, looked back again with impotent rage at Freda.

Then, with a final obscene gesture to her, he marched out. The inspector followed, leaving the door wide open.

Howard went over and collected his

document case from the desk. Then he and Janet went out together, neither of them looking at Freda. They left the door open.

Freda stared after them for a moment, then went over and savagely kicked the door shut. After lighting herself a cigarette, she went over to the sideboard and prescribed herself a generous measure of gin.

She was thoughtful, worried. But after a moment, a smile of satisfaction grew around her mouth. Putting down her unfinished gin on the desk, she put the drawer back in its place.

Then, going to the metal figure, she took it off its pedestal and placed it on the floor.

The top of the pedestal was hollow. She took out four hundred pounds, and replaced the metal figure.

She laughed to herself, handling the notes lovingly. Going back to her gin, she was thoughtful for a while, then her expression brightened.

'Inspector Robin won't be worried about me,' she told herself. 'Not now he's got Leonard Black.'

She laughed and slapped the bundle of notes on the desk.

'That's it! Finish. All over . . . ' She broke off her train of thought, smiling. 'Nice bath, I think. Wash it all away.'

Catching sight of Howard's picture, she crossed to it and slammed it face-down.

Sitting down at the desk, she finished the gin and her cigarette. After stubbing it out, she rose languidly and returned her glass to the sideboard, switching on the radio. It was tuned to a musical station.

She was on her way to the bathroom when, above the noise of the radio, she heard the insistent ringing of the doorbell.

Startled, she stopped dead.

Then, thinking 'How silly!', she crossed and opened the door.

The Tops T.V. engineer was standing there, smiling. His firm's logo was emblazoned on the back of his service jacket. He explained who he was, and Freda admitted him.

As she crossed to show him where to go, her hip brushed the pedestal with the metal figure on, causing it to wobble and almost topple. With a quick grab, the young man rescued the figure from damage.

Freda turned, only to see him with the figure raised in his hand.

She gasped, irrational fears flashing through her agitated mind. He was going to murder her! Quickly, she realised that her fears were groundless.

The young man was surprised at Freda's reaction. Surely no ornament could be *that* valuable? Or was she a lunatic?

Carefully, he replaced the metal figure.

Feeling a little foolish, she showed the man over to the set, and he began to service it.

Freda picked up the transistor radio, still playing, and went into the bathroom.

Left alone, the young man fiddled with the set for a moment or two, and then his manner completely altered.

Quickly, he looked about the place, then crept to the bedrooms' doors and made sure nobody was in either of them. Likewise, the kitchen. Then he went and listened at the alcove leading to the bathroom.

The radio continued to play, and he could hear Freda singing along to it, above the splashing sounds of the running taps.

Satisfied he had a clear field, he set to work quickly.

Taking the lighter and cigarettes from the table, he put them into his pocket. Next, he hurried into both bedrooms, bringing out anything of value that he could find and popping it into his bag.

He repeated his thievery along the mantelshelf, sweeping more objects into his bag.

When he came to the desk, he could hardly believe his eyes.

Swiftly into his bag went Freda's jewellery, followed by the money — all four hundred pounds of it. He whipped off his jacket and stuffed that in as well.

He was just leaving when he saw Freda's mink coat on the rack.

He grabbed it, rolled it up, then found that he was unable to fit it into the now-bulging bag.

Reluctant to leave it, he quickly put it on. Then, after a look at himself in the mirror, he left the room, smirking.

The radio continued to play for a few minutes, then stopped.

Silence.

Freda emerged from the bathroom, dressed in nothing but a bath towel.

She gasped loudly as she saw that the man had gone. She rushed across to the desk, and her gasp turned into a sob of rage.

'Help! Help! Police!'

She started to dash out, then gave a scream as some eighteen inches of the towel became trapped on the inside of the door.

She came back, reclaiming the towel, and her decency. She slammed the door and raced to the buzzer, switched it on.

'Ernie! Ernie!' She listened . . . and listened . . . 'Not there!' She swore luridly. 'Over at that blasted pub again!'

Sobbing quietly, she hung up, and sank slowly to her knees.

'Can't bloody win, can you . . . ?'

The Shrine

The bell clanged suddenly, startlingly. Madame Cordier did not move in her chair. Perhaps because she did not hear it above the moan of the wind and the splash of rain that beat upon the poor Taverne du Soleil. Or perhaps because she did not want to be disturbed from her half-sleep, her musing . . .

The bell clanged once more. Loudly and insistently, it reverberated in her ears. Its echoes lingered in the shabby and unkempt room. With a curse, Madame Cordier roused herself from her stupor.

'*Sacré Nom!* Who can that be? At this hour of the night!' She shivered and drew her shawl closer to her thin, bent body. 'Some traveller lost in this accursed storm — '

She sat listening for a moment.

'Ah, well — I will call Pepi. He shall see who it is.' Her voice rose in a screech, 'Pepi! Pepi! Awake, you fool! There is someone at the door!' At that moment, the bell clanged again. Madame's voice cracked with sudden rage. *'Diable!* Cannot you hear, Pepi? You sleeping pig! Wake up! Hurry! Hurry! Curse you for a slow-witted idiot! Quick, I say — or this clanging will crack my ears!'

There was a shuffling behind the staircase door. A sleepy voice grumbled, and Pepi opened the door and approached the woman. In the light of the hanging oil-lamp he seemed like some evil apparition. He was squat, and his long, muscular arms gave him a gorilla-like appearance,

'Who can it be, Madame? Ringing at this late hour? Never do honest travellers call so late as this — '

The bell broke into his words with greater violence than before. The caller would not, it seemed, be denied admission to the Taverne du Soleil. Madame turned upon her servant savagely, twisting her body round in her chair.

'Sacré Nom! Go, I say, see who it is!'

'But it may be thieves who ring — or murderers!' Pepi spoke nervously.

Madame burst into a shrill cackle.

'Ha, ha! Thieves! And what should thieves want with my poor inn? And if they be murderers — what of it, eh, Pepi? It would avail them little to murder me, or a poor half-wit like you! Ha, ha!' Pepi shuddered, and the woman cackled again.

'But it is better to wait, Madame Cordier — '

'*Crénom!* You are afraid!'

Yet again the bell clanged. Its peals were followed by loud blows upon the door. Madame covered her ears and screeched at her servant to go and open it.

'If it be the Devil himself, let him in! Go, quickly — I cannot bear this noise! Go, before it clangs again!'

With nervous and hurried steps, Pepi shuffled out to admit the traveller. Madame relaxed in her chair.

'Ah! If only my poor brother Gaston were here!' she muttered. 'He would not be afraid of thieves or murderers — Not he, my beloved Gaston . . . ' Her voice trailed off into a moan.

There was a sound of bolts being

drawn. The noise of the storm swept into the room, then died away as the door closed. Then came voices: Pepi's, nervous and childish, and the deep rough notes of a man's voice. Their footsteps approached, and then the traveller entered, with Pepi following.

The stranger was of medium height, heavily-built, between forty and fifty. He was darkly bearded and his left arm was missing from the shoulder. He stood blinking in the dim light, the rain dripping from his coat and from his hat. He pulled his hat off and greeted the woman. 'Good evening, Madame.'

Pepi held two travelling bags, and smiled as he said:

'It is a gentleman who seeks a bed for the night, Madame. He is lost — a traveller from Marseilles — '

The woman ignored the man's greeting. She peered at him short-sightedly. The man went on, in a voice that held a queer, nervous note in its depths, as if it restrained a strong emotion.

'That is right! From Marseilles, Madame — and lost in this storm! I found your inn by good chance. *Mon Dieu!* But what a night it is out there on the road! I am sorry to have disturbed you, and to have made so much noise. But I am so tired — I must rest for the night — '

Madame Cordier gave him a somewhat surly answer.

'We are not used to travellers here — and the hour is late. But you can have a bed in the room above, if you wish. It has not been slept in since my poor brother slept there — ten years ago.'

'I am most grateful, Madame — '

'*Hélas! Mon pauvre Gaston!*' went on the woman, forgetting the man before her for a moment in her obsession, whilst the stranger watched her, his shadowed face grave and still. 'Poor, poor brother! Drowned in such a storm as this. He and my husband — a low pig of a man — it was not for him I wept, but poor Gaston!' Her voice trailed off into a low moan.

Suddenly she screamed at Pepi: 'Imbecile! Help the gentleman with his coat! Standing here like a block of wood!

Quick, take his coat and hat to the kitchen to dry!'

Pepi started at her voice and quickly helped the man to remove his coat. He went out hurriedly to the kitchen with the garments. The man stood revealed in shabby clothes. He pulled a chair close to Madame Cordier and sat looking at her.

The woman's head was sunk on her breast. She was oblivious of his presence and muttered to herself. The man looked almost furtively round the room and noted its squalor. Then his gaze returned to the woman, and he sighed a little. Pepi returned from the kitchen and stood aimlessly beside the man. Suddenly Madame saw him,

'Go on, Pepi! Take the gentleman's bags to his room! Would you stand there all night? *Sacré Nom!* Must I be plagued forever with such a fool as you?'

Quickly, Pepi gathered up the two bags. '*Oui, Madame!* I go! I prepare his bed — *oui, oui!*' And he shuffled up the stairs, closing the staircase door after him.

The stranger smiled. '*Bien! Mon Dieu,* but I am weary! All the way from

Marseilles . . . now and then a friendly lift, but walking most of the time.'

The woman asked disinterestedly: 'Where are you going?'

The other paused for a moment before he replied. As he spoke, he eyed her intently.

'That, Madame, I cannot tell you — now.' He smiled to himself for a moment. 'It is a strange journey upon which I have set out. Ah! A happy journey, too. And the end — the end of the journey is so very near . . . '

Madame Cordier relapsed into her obsession once more, murmuring in a low wail to herself:

'*Mon pauvre Gaston* — *his* journey ended so sadly! To be cast into the cold, raging sea. To be at the mercy of the savage storm. Cold, cold sea! To drown — ah, *nom de Dieu!* What could be more terrible than that?'

'And your poor husband, too?' The man put the question to her quietly. For a moment, the woman did not realise that he was talking to her. Then she said:

'Bah! Him? I'm glad he died. I could

not have borne it if he had lived!'

'They were together when they died?'

Madame ignored his question. She muttered to herself again. Then suddenly, she became conscious of his presence. 'But you are hungry? You would eat and drink?'

'Thank you, no, Madame. I am too weary to eat. I will take a little wine when I go to bed.'

The woman nodded. 'You will sleep well, I think. The bed is big and comfortable — would that my Gaston slept in it now — but he sleeps on the bed of the sea . . . '

The other shook his head slowly. There was a tenderness in his voice, '*Hélas!* It is sad that brave men should die.'

The woman did not answer. For a moment there was silence in the room. Outside, the storm plucked at the old inn with greedy fingers.

'And, now?' asked the traveller. 'You look after the inn?'

'*Oui*, monsieur. But it is hard. Our custom has dwindled away. Once we were prosperous, many travellers sought our roof. But during the last ten years, all that has died. You are the first to shelter here for longer than my poor brain can remember,'

'That is bad — '

She gestured towards her feet. 'And my legs are dead — I cannot attend to things as I did.'

The man shook his head in sympathy. And then the woman's voice lowered to a whisper. She muttered to herself, rocking her head from side to side in misery.

'The shrine! There is the little shrine I would make in memory of Gaston — but I have no money — ' Her whisper faded pitifully, like a child's. There was silence once more. A tiny shadow of a smile seemed to play about the man's mouth.

'It is hard to be poor, Madame. But, never mind! Perhaps there is a good time coming for you, eh? Who knows what *le bon Dieu* has in store for us? You may yet have your shrine for poor Gaston. And perhaps you may even burn a little candle for your husband — ' And the man's smile grew wider, to fade again.

'Never!' exclaimed the woman, with

sudden passion. '*He* can rot with the Devil! A swaggering, drunken pig was André my husband! And Gaston — so kind, so gentle — ' Her voice became a whispered moan once more. The man regarded her keenly. Again the smile flickered across his lips, this time a little twisted.

'Do not weep for the dead. The quick and the dead shall meet, so soon — so soon.'

He leaned across to the woman. There was a new tenseness in his attitude, in his voice, which did not communicate itself to her.

'Besides, Madame . . . ' He weighed each word carefully as it fell from his lips. He watched her face as carefully as he spoke. ' . . . sometimes, sometimes — those we give up for dead . . . return. Mistakes are sometimes made, and after a few years have passed, loved ones — ' His voice faltered a little on the two words. ' — return. A little changed, perhaps, but alive and well.'

The woman did not answer. She seemed unaware of his presence, even.

226

Her head was sunk on her breast, rocking to and fro gently. Her eyes were closed. The stranger pursued his subject.

'Why, I myself have heard of men lost at sea and believed dead, who have been saved; who have found fortune in a foreign country, and who have later returned to their joyful families.'

Madame opened her eyes and looked at him. The man drew back. His bearded face was cast over more darkly by shadow. Shaking her head, she replied:

'Ha! They are dreams you talk of! Fairy tales!'

The man looked at her fixedly for a second. Then, shrugging his shoulders, he replied:

'Ah, well, who knows? One day, perhaps, your Gaston — or your so-unpleasant husband — may return to you after all.'

'You mock me! You talk foolishly!' the woman said, her voice savage and bitter.

Silence again fell upon the two. The man watched her speculatively. The woman's eyes were closed. The wind howled round the inn like some lost wild thing. Involuntarily, the man yawned and rubbed his eyes with the knuckles of his one hand.

Then, noiselessly, the staircase door swung open slowly. The man did not hear it. Did not know that Pepi stood framed in the doorway, looking at him. Pepi's face had changed. It no longer bore an expression of childishness. It was malignantly inhuman. In his eyes there was a terrible look of cunning. His mouth was open and greedy. And as suddenly and silently, he pulled the door close and was hidden from sight.

The stranger yawned once more, this time noisily.

'*Mon Dieu!* How welcome your bed will be, Madame — I shall sleep forever, I think!'

Madame opened her eyes. 'You must indeed be weary.' She raised her voice in a screech. 'Pepi! Pepi! You slow idiot — come down, the gentleman is waiting. Hurry, imbecile!'

There was a muffled response from above and the sound of feet shuffling down the stairs. In a moment, the servant descended into the room,

'All is prepared for monsieur?' asked Madame.

Pepi's face was expressionless as he answered the woman.

'*Mais oui*, Madame Cordier — all is ready. A candle burns in monsieur's room. His soft bed awaits him.'

With a smile of anticipation, the man rose slowly, smothering a yawn.

'*Bien!* Then I will bid you goodnight, Madame Cordier. And you, Pepi, you will bring me a glass of red wine — a nightcap, eh?' He smiled sleepily at Pepi, and the servant's eyes were black with cunning as he replied: '*Certainement*, monsieur.'

'*Bien*, Pepi! Goodnight, Madame!'

Madame did not reply. The man waited for a moment for her to speak, then slowly crossed to the stairs and ascended them heavily with exclamations of weariness. Pepi stood at foot of the stairs watching him, on his face a crafty grin.

Then, when the man had disappeared from sight, he pushed the door closed, and with an animal-like movement crossed to Madame. He spoke into her ear with an excited, hoarse whisper.

'Madame Cordier!'

'What is it? Hurry with the wine for monsieur!'

'A moment, Madame! Pepi is slow, stupid, *mais oui* — but not so stupid as you think!'

'What do you mean?' Madame spoke impatiently.

Pepi's mouth was close to her ear. 'The traveller upstairs — he is not what you think: he is no poor traveller. For in one of his bags, Madame, he has thousands of francs!'

'What? Imbecile! What are you saying?'

'It is true!' Pepi's voice was urgent. 'How much money he has, I cannot say for certain — I count but slowly. But the bag is stuffed with money — much money! I have felt the crisp notes with my fingers — bundles of them!' His fingers curled into claws. Then he pulled an object from his pocket. It was a thin silver chain with a little cross attached to it. He dangled it before the woman.

'And there is jewellery, too! Look, Madame!'

Madame's breath was coming in broken gasps. She took the chain in her bony fingers and scrutinized it closely. Suddenly she started and held it closer to her dimmed eyes. Her voice shook with deep agitation.

'*Sacré Nom!* But — but — I know this chain — this cross!' Her fingers pulled at it convulsively, as if she would tear its secret from the inanimate metal. '*Diable!* I cannot see . . . You, Pepi, you see if there is writing.'

Pepi took the cross and chain from her trembling hands. He, too, peered closely at it in the dim light.

'*Oui*, Madame, there is writing on the back of the cross. It is very worn — '

'Read it, Pepi! Read it!' Her voice rose in an excited screech.

For a moment, the servant looked at the cross. Then, slowly and with difficulty, he read the inscription:

'A — N — D — R — André.'

'*Sacré Nom!* André!'

'*Oui* Madame, there is more; de M

— A — R — Marie — '

'Ah-h-h!' Madame Cordier's voice rose in a thin scream. '*André!* My husband — it is he — ' Her fingers twisted themselves round the chain again as she took it from Pepi. He stood silent, mouth agape, unable to comprehend the situation.

'*Crénom!* How did I not know? Ah, the beard! The arm! Curse him! Curse him! He has come to gloat over me in my misery! André! Back from the dead — incredible!'

Her voice had risen in a paroxysm of rage. Now it sank into a murmur as she lay back in her chair, overcome by the shock. 'André — alive, and with thousands of francs in his bag — is that not so, Pepi?'

Pepi answered her with eagerness. '*Oui*, Madame! Enough to buy us food and wine, food and clothes!'

The woman interrupted him harshly. 'André will give us none!'

But the servant continued, his voice soft and curiously compelling in quality. 'Enough, Madame, for you to make a shrine for poor, poor brother Gaston . . . '

There was a silence. The room suddenly took upon itself another atmosphere. Before, it had been squalid and wretched; now it seemed hideously menacing. Even the storm which still raged outside offered more security, more humanness . . .

The woman moaned again. 'André will give us nothing!'

And then Pepi said: 'Give? But why should we not *take* — ?'

Madame Cordier did not reply. She sat tensed in her chair, silent and thinking, turning over Pepi's suggestion in her mind. Presently, she murmured, half to herself: 'We might steal a little — a few hundred francs — '

'A little? *Mais non* — we must have *all* or none!' Pepi's words pounced on her savagely.

She shook her head wearily. 'You are foolish, *mon Pepi*! Tomorrow, when he wakes, he would soon discover his loss.'

'*If* he wakes, Madame . . . '

Madame started. She raised her eyes to his slowly. The cruel intent in their black depths sent a shudder through her. '*Mon Dieu!*' she moaned quickly. 'No! Not that!'

Her voice died away and was drowned by the servant's eager words. He spoke quickly, with devilish command.

'You hate your husband! Always have you done so! When you thought him dead, you were glad! It is only brother Gaston you love. Now the man you hate has returned to mock you, to gloat over your misery!' Grimly, relentlessly, he went on. 'Let him go back — back to the dead — and we will profit by his return!'

'No, no! I cannot!'

Again the other voice cut into her fading whisper. His eyes watched her with a terrible, hypnotising stare.

'The shrine . . . ' Pepi said.

And she repeated the word after him, slowly, softly. Then: 'For Gaston . . . '

A smile of triumph swept over Pepi's face. There was a pause. Their eyes held each other's, almost as if they we lovers. Then Pepi's head turned towards the kitchen. Quietly, purposely, he shuffled to it and disappeared. Madame watched the door through which he had gone. In a moment he returned, and she could not choke back the cry as she saw the cruel knife held in one hand. He smiled at her.

'No one knows of him, Madame! Before dawn, I will take the body and hide it forever.' He indicated a wine-glass he carried in his other hand. 'I will blind him with this pepper — and then — ' He crossed to the staircase door. He opened it, then turned to the woman. 'It is well?'

Madame Cordier nodded. Pepi ascended the stairs. He called out: 'I bring your red wine, monsieur — ' And there was a sleepy murmur in reply.

The woman sat, her chin sunk on her breast, and crooning childishly to herself.

'The shrine — candles burning — *mon pauvre Gaston* — '

She did not seem to hear the scream from the room above. She muttered still as there came the sounds of struggling. A voice called in agony, a body crashed to the floor, and there were curses from Pepi. Then a voice called: 'Help! Save me! My sister! Murder! My sister, Marie!'

The woman ceased her muttering and gave a cry.

There was the sound of stumbling on the stairs and, groaning, the traveller appeared at the doorway. His face was splashed with the pepper. Blood ran from a wound in his chest. He reeled blindly and called out:

'It is I — Gaston! It is your brother, come back to you — tomorrow, I would have revealed myself!'

Madame was making convulsive movements in her chair. She could not move from it, and she cried in her agony to the man.

'André saved me,' he called to her, 'he gave me the little cross before he died!'

Above the woman's shrieks of: 'Gaston! My Gaston!' came the shouts of the incensed Pepi. Gaston heard his approach.

'Quickly, save me! I cannot see, and Pepi comes to murder me!'

His scream drowned Madame's cry. Pepi descended and drove the knife into Gaston's back with all the force of his impetus as he rushed down the stairs.

As Gaston crumpled, gurgling, to the floor, Madame burst into an insane cackle, and collapsed in her chair. Pepi stood over the body, his mouth twisted in a grin of triumph.

The woman's crazed laughter died into a gentle murmuring.

'The shrine ... *mon pauvre Gaston* ... candles burning ...'

And outside, the wind moaned and the rain spattered against the old windows of the Taverne du Soleil as if the storm would rage forever.

The Passenger

Seven o'clock was chalked on the call-board in the narrow hall of Robinson's Commercial Hotel, Hull; and at seven o'clock on the dot, on that autumn Friday morning, the chamber-maid knocked at No. 7 and went into the room. She put the tray on the slightly rickety bedside table and the enamel hot-water jug on the washstand, drew back the curtains and went out, closing the door behind her quietly.

Mr. Ellis yawned himself awake, got out of bed, and sat on the edge of it to drink his morning tea. His sleep-filled eyes took in the small room, with its wallpaper of hummingbirds and flowers and trellis-work. The shining linoleum on the floor, and the worn strip of carpet beside the bed, upon which he had placed his feet, curling his toes.

Presently he stood, a weedy little figure in pyjama trousers and vest, before the washstand mirror and shaved from the hot-water jug. A little while later he was descending the stairs, wearing his neat, dark grey pinstripe suit and a clean white collar with a quiet tie, his black shoes well-polished.

'Mr. Ellis's breakfast!' fat Mrs. Robinson called down to the kitchen, and Mr. Ellis went into the dining room. He hadn't much time to linger, and Mrs. Robinson saw to it that he did not have to wait a moment between finishing his porridge and starting on the haddock and poached egg.

The several other commercial travellers staying at the hotel had not put in an appearance yet. Mr. Ellis was making an early start; he planned to get in twenty or more calls before he headed the nose of his little car south.

He was a senior traveller for the London hardware firm he represented. Twenty years he'd been with them, and his connections were established: it wasn't often that he had to work new lines onto new customers. To most of those he called on, he was an old friend, whose word was his bond that the product he was selling was everything he cracked it up to be.

Not that Mr. Ellis ever attempted to crack up his firm's products too much. His methods were more subtle than that. Flashing his winning smile on and off at suitable moments, he would keep his voice to a moderate tone, always a little quieter and slower than the customer's. When he paused, it was not because he was stuck for want of something to say, it was for dramatic effect.

He knew his customers thoroughly, their illnesses and afflictions, their moods. He never argued — the customer might not always be right, but there was no dice in winning the argument only to lose the sale.

His suitcase carefully packed and in the boot of his car, he set off. Mr. Ellis's working day had begun. Ahead of him lay shops. Shops in side-streets, mixed up with newsagents and hairdressers, butchers and fish-and-chip cafés; shops which sold firewood and paraffin, birdseed and candles; shops in the slums; shops in the discreet suburbs; larger shops in the high streets, noisy with traffic and streams of shoppers.

And then, around three o'clock, he would set out for London and home.

Mr. Ellis did not feel even the faintest twinge of premonition as he turned his left-hand-drive two-seater with the hood up out of the street in which Robinson's Commercial Hotel stood. He had no knowledge that he was destined never to see London or his home again.

* * *

Harry saw the left-hand-drive two-seater with the hood up just outside Chelmsford at about five o'clock, and thumbed a lift. A bit of an autumn mist creeping in from the North Sea added to the gloom of the approaching night, and Mr. Ellis had got in all his calls very satisfactorily and was in a generous frame of mind.

He was also talkative; he usually was after a day's work. Harry did his best to appear interested, but his big, heavily-jowled face was sombre. Mr. Ellis gave

244

him one or two opportunities to open up about himself, but Harry just said that he'd missed the Chelmsford-to-London coach and he wanted to get to London quickly. 'My father's sick, over in Bermondsey,' he said. Mr. Ellis made appropriately commiserating noises.

All Harry wanted was to put as many miles as fast as possible between himself and the house with the shrubbery-lined drive up to the front door. The house which he'd cased the past week, on the outskirts of Chelmsford. The house where the old chap was lying in the hall, his bald head bashed in. He was positive no one had seen him enter or leave, so there'd be no squawk till the old boy's housekeeper returned from the local cinema. She went to the pictures every Friday afternoon — Harry had found that out. That was why he'd picked that afternoon for the job.

Mr. Ellis chattered on. 'Been on the road over twenty years; right up the East Coast as far as Hull, I take in. To earn good money as a salesman you've got to do a full day's work. I've made twenty-two calls today. That'll mean a couple of quid added to my weekly basic of seven pounds ten.'

He worked his way round to his favourite story of the old girl during the war, pleading for a saucepan. ''Do you know what I'm reduced to boiling my cabbages in?' she said. 'A tin chamber-pot!' Nearly crying, she was. Yes, I'd have driven a hundred miles to find the old girl a saucepan. But of course you couldn't get one then for love or money.'

When he'd exhausted his stock of commercial travellers' tales, Mr. Ellis began yarning about the variety of cars that had been through his hands during the past twenty years.

'There was an old Model T I once had,' he said. 'Do you know, I had to drive it uphill backwards because of the gravity feed. It's the truth I'm telling you.'

He glanced at his passenger's large, thick hands lying inertly on his knees. His hands were greenish pale under the dashboard-light. They were muscular, their fingers brown with cigarette-stain.

Harry said he was a mechanic.

Harry's thoughts were back at the house, while Mr. Ellis went off on the reason for his flea of a car having a left-hand drive; and how, when he'd first bought it, he had thought he would have a heap of trouble driving it — used as he was, of course, to a right-hand drive — but he'd found it easy enough.

And so it went, Mr. Ellis chatting away, as the headlights burrowed through the deepening night.

And Harry thinking he could hole up in London: there was no place like the big smoke to hole up in. Look at it any way, he didn't see how it could be pinned on him.

He'd left nothing behind, he was sure of that: no fingerprints, nothing that would point to him. The way he had forced the window — any passing tramp might have done that.

The wads of currency notes crackled in his inside pocket, and in his hip-pocket when he eased his heavy frame in his seat. He'd taken a quick count; he was sure there was three hundred nicker there.

Suddenly it hit him. This wasn't like any of the other jobs he'd been on the run from, this was different. It was murder he was running away from this time. He hadn't meant to do in the old boy. Why did the old fool have to wake up from his afternoon nap?

Murder wouldn't mean just another stretch of the sort he'd been used to. He started to sweat. It suddenly felt hot in the little car. He fought back the impulse to shout to the man beside him to stop and let him out so that he could run. Run away from the black, choking terror that awaited him.

He didn't notice that the car had forked left, that they'd left the A12.

'That was Brentwood,' Mr. Ellis said. Harry remembered that they had come through a town. 'This is the road to Tilbury.'

Harry jerked his head round and stared at him.

'For the ferry, like I said. I go as far as Lewisham,' Mr. Ellis said. 'That's where I live. Then the rest of it is yours. You'll get a bus easy enough.'

Harry nodded. His thoughts churned like a mill-race. Would the big smoke be so easy for him to hide up in now? Now it was murder? If only he could get farther away, get himself an alibi.

He thought of his brother in Cardiff. He hadn't seen him since they'd been demobbed. Ed would help him, though. Ed would say he'd been with him in Cardiff all the time. And how much further could you get from Chelmsford than Cardiff?

Mr. Ellis had grown quiet. He had exhausted his fund of stories, and had given up trying to draw out his passenger. Now his thoughts were flying ahead of the speeding car like pigeons homing.

From the long hill they were descending, Mr. Ellis could see a familiar cluster of lights in the distance. Out of the lights, he could see a tall yellow funnel rising. 'Tilbury Docks,' he said without turning his head.

Abstractedly, Harry kept his gaze on the lights, which seemed to dance and sparkle along the dockside. Beyond the gleam of water, strung out against the darkness, lay more lights.

'Gravesend,' Mr. Ellis said.

But Harry's spinning thoughts had suddenly focussed on an idea. The car. That was all he needed. If he had the car, he could drive like hell all through the night to Cardiff. Then Ed could help him fix himself up all right.

He glanced at the dashboard clock. Just on seven o'clock. He could make Cardiff before midnight.

'Be there in a few minutes,' Mr. Ellis said. 'Ferry leaves at seven-sixteen.'

The car's headlamps lit up the high walls on either side of the lonely, narrowly winding road. Desperately, Harry toyed with getting the other to stop the car now, he could deal with him quick, then drive on. But the sweeping headlights of cars coming from the docks and those overtaking them made it too risky.

They were driving through Tilbury's streets, and then up an incline. A sudden squall drove off the river and threw itself at the little car. Harry glimpsed notices: *To the Docks*. One said: *Vehicular Ferry*.

Now they stopped by a ticket-office.

Mr. Ellis got out.

'I'll buy your ticket,' he said to his passenger. 'You can settle up on board.'

Harry watched him go to the ticket-office window. There was a woman behind the window who handed him the tickets. A moment or two later, he was back in the car. 'You hold these,' Mr. Ellis said, and Harry took the three pieces of pasteboard.

The ferry-boat lay against the dockside, waiting. Mr. Ellis slowed the car with practised efficiency into bottom gear as they went aboard. The deck was packed with assorted cars and vans, overshadowed by a couple of lorries. Mr. Ellis edged his car into what seemed to be the last space that was left on the crowded deck. They were in the shadow of one of the lorries, near the vessel's side.

Mr. Ellis opened the car door and got out. As he got out to follow him, Harry noticed that he did not take out the ignition-key. They stood near the car. The deck was rocking a little and the wind, salt and cold, whipped between the vessels surrounding them. The ship's engines rumbled beneath them.

Mr. Ellis moved to watch the figures on the dimly lighted dockside. Ropes slithered like black snakes. Harry moved with him. Overhead the sky was starless. Beside him, Mr. Ellis turned, and Harry caught the greenish glint of his watch-face in the darkness.

'Seven-sixteen on the dot,' Mr. Ellis said. 'Always is. Ten minutes and we'll be at Gravesend, then heading for home.'

Harry glanced about him. The two of them were masked from the bridge by the lorry, and from anyone on deck by a motor-van.

The vessel swung out into the river; the engines began to settle down with a steady, deep-throated throb. The wind-squalls drove more strongly into their faces.

Harry turned and gave a quick look over the side.

Now they were about halfway across the river. Upstream, against the twinkling lights of Tilbury, fast receding, he glimpsed the dark shadow of a steamship moving gracefully against the background of the lighted shore.

He raised his right hand, the fingers extended and close together, thumb upright and wrist locked. Mr. Ellis glanced up for a moment, the man beside him seemed to tower over him. Then Harry brought the hard edge of his hand in a lightning blow against Mr. Ellis's windpipe, just below the Adam's apple.

He was dead as Harry caught his sagging body and, masking him with his own bulk, lifted him clean over the side. He held on to the limp, dangling figure's coat-collar. Then Harry eased his grip until he clutched the other's coat-sleeve with one hand. For a moment, Mr. Ellis's weedy shape dangled against the ship's side.

Then a gentle tearing sound, and the coat-sleeve came away from the coat. There was a quiet splash as Mr. Ellis's body hit the water and disappeared. Harry let the coat-sleeve drift down. It floated against the ship's side like a dark pennant.

He stood there trembling all over, bathed in perspiration, waiting for some cry of alarm. But there was nothing: only the noise of the ship's engines and the squalls from the river.

He turned back to the car. He glimpsed the glow of a cigarette-end in the lorry cabin as he got into the driving seat.

The gentle rocking of the ferryboat ceased as it lay alongside the pier at Gravesend. Already the vehicles were starting up in readiness to go ashore. Harry switched on the ignition-key. An icy shock assailed him when he pressed the starter-button and nothing happened.

He pressed again: still nothing. For a moment his brain was numbed. Then he pulled out the choke and pressed the starter-button again. A great wave of relief flooded him as the engine started up.

Cars and vans were moving off, over the ramp on to the dockside and up the slope towards the town. Harry edged the car behind the lorry, and now he was heading up the slope towards the ticket-office. The lorry drove off and Harry slowed up the car as the uniformed figure loomed up in the dim light. Harry leaned across, lowered the off-side window, and held out the tickets.

Harry watched the man scrutinize the tickets, then saw him glance into the car.

The man started to say something, but Harry didn't wait to hear. Something in the ticket-collector's expression filled him with a sudden ungovernable panic. He'd slipped up somewhere; he knew it.

There was a grating screech as he fumbled changing gears, shooting up the narrow street ahead of him. He turned right at the top of the street and sped through the town in the direction of London. Drive as fast as he could, that was his only hope; bypass London and head westwards for Cardiff.

The police car appeared out of nowhere just as Harry was approaching Sydenham. They drew alongside and edged him against the pavement, and there was nothing for Harry to do but to stop.

'It might just as well be us as anyone else,' he was told. 'Every patrol round London has got your number from Gravesend.'

Later, when he'd told them all they wanted to know, one of the detectives said: 'And to think that if you hadn't done such a silly thing you might have got away with it.'

Harry looked at him blankly.

'Handing over three tickets,' said the detective. 'When you should have only had two: one for the car and one for yourself. Where was your passenger?'

The Frightened Client

Our taxi swung over the bridge and presently turned between two great iron gates into a wide drive. A grey mist drifted up from the river, and in the dusk the trees on either side loomed up, dark and towering. As we rounded a bend I saw the house ahead of us, low and rambling. Its windows stared unlighted on either side of a heavy portico; and the whole appearance of the place was, I thought, distinctly uninviting.

I said to Mr. Brett: 'Cosy little place.'

He turned his long saturnine face, limned by the glow of his cigarette, towards me, but made no comment. I glanced at my watch. We'd certainly got a move on since Mr. Brett received that somewhat odd phone call something under half-an-hour back. I happened to be in his office when it came through, jotting down some routine notes for attention next day, and took the call. It was a woman.

'I would like to speak to Mr. Brett. My name is Mrs. Guy Cavendish and the matter is urgent — '

It was a cultured voice, though a trifle taut with an undercurrent of fear. When you've been tagging along with a private detective, you begin to learn how to place voices that come at you over the phone. Mrs. Cavendish was worried, I got that the first time. But, of course, she wasn't the first character to come on the line with a note of apprehension in the voice. I knew from experience she might have nothing more awful on her mind than a pet poodle that'd been pinched, or some pretty bauble lost between the latest nightclub and a Mayfair flat. So, with my best businesslike intonation, I'd said: 'If you'll hold on, I'll see if Mr. Brett can speak to you.' My hand over the receiver, I had said to him: 'A Mrs. Guy Cavendish.'

He had shown a certain amount of interest. 'Sounds expensive. Giving her husband's first name means she thinks she's important.'

'She's up in the air about something.'

'She wouldn't be ringing me if she wasn't. Maybe I'll mention my fee and bring her down to earth like a shot pigeon.' And, with a grin, he'd taken his feet off the desk and grabbed the phone. 'Martin Brett speaking.'

I gathered from the way he answered her that she wanted to see him soon as he could make it at her house. He said the address over for me to write down. I could hear her voice blurred over the wire, because she wasn't speaking quietly, and Mr. Brett had held the receiver away from his ear a little. Then suddenly there'd sounded a queer, choky sort of gasp, and her voice had stopped, sending a horrid prickly sensation under my scalp. There'd been a click of the phone at the other end being replaced, and silence. Mr. Brett had flashed his receiver but nothing happened. Mrs. Cavendish hadn't come on the line again.

Lighting a cigarette, Mr. Brett had said slowly, 'We could do something about it, or we could leave it alone.'

'Maybe she just changed her mind.' It was late, and I wanted to shut up the office and go home.

'Not so fast. She had to ring off in the middle of a sentence.' I hadn't been able to find the answer to that one, so I'd shrugged and waited to see what he would do about it, praying he would drop it and decide to go off for a drink or two instead. But he said: 'Somehow, I have the idea there should be something in this for me.'

★ ★ ★

After that, the action had been pretty snappy. I'd barely had time to lock the office and dive after Mr. Brett into a taxi. On the way, during the relatively calm moments when we hadn't been alternatively braking or accelerating with what I considered to be sadistic violence on the driver's part, I'd managed to learn that Mrs. Cavendish hadn't got around to giving Mr. Brett any notion of what was on her mind before her sudden and somewhat sinister silence. 'I merely

262

gathered she was scared of something or someone; that was all.'

'Maybe the danger was even more imminent than she'd realised?'

But he'd merely lit another cigarette and gone into a huddle with himself in the corner of the taxi. So now here we were, drawing up outside Mrs. Cavendish's house, and I was wondering what might lie beyond that heavy, studded front door. Maybe Mr. Brett was wasting his time and I had been right when I'd suggested Mrs. Cavendish had just suddenly changed her mind?

Mr. Brett paid off the taxi, which drove off and left us with the silence unbroken but for the steady drip-drip of the mist-laden trees around us.

'Not what you might call the welcome mat laid out,' I said. I was wondering why no one had heard our arrival and opened the door to us.

'You forget — ' He smiled bleakly. ' — we are a trifle unexpected.' I pressed the large bell-push and heard the ring reverberate somewhere beyond.

Mr. Brett observed: 'You could have

saved it, Gorgeous; the door's open.'

I started, and forgot to make my usual chilling response to his sardonic familiarity as I saw the door move an inch wider. I hadn't noticed in the gloom that it wasn't properly closed. I looked at him questioningly. He promptly shoved the door fully open and I followed him in. As we stood in the hall, the shadowed gloom was suddenly illuminated from a chandelier overhead. At the foot of the stairs a woman faced us, her hand on a light-switch. She was tall and heavy-featured, and stared at us suspiciously.

'How did you get in here?' Her voice was harsh, with the slight trace of a foreign accent.

Mr. Brett nodded over his shoulder at the open door. 'I'll give you three guesses.' He smiled.

Her face didn't relax. 'Who are you? What do you want?'

'No,' Mr. Brett said genially, 'you tell me. Who are *you* and what do *you* want?'

She stared at him, then muttered impatiently, 'I am secretary-companion to

Mrs. Cavendish. Again, I must ask you: what do you want?'

'Since you insist on being so helpful, perhaps you'd just go along to Mrs. Cavendish, tell her Mr. Brett's here.'

'Is she expecting you?'

'I think she'll remember the name,' was his reply.

The other turned to eye me. Mr. Brett interpreted her glance and said: 'This delectable lady is *my* secretary. I prefer 'em,' he added with gratuitous candour, 'to be decorative.'

The woman turned abruptly and walked quickly beyond the wide staircase. She paused at a door and went in, closing it behind her.

I said: 'You know, I somehow think she doesn't care for us.'

He nodded. 'You know, I somehow think you're right.'

'Think Mrs. Cavendish'll see us?'

'Depends what made her cut that phone call.'

I was watching the door, waiting for the tall woman to reappear. A silence lay over the house, a silence you could have cut with a pair of scissors. The door opened suddenly and the woman stood there.

'Mrs. Cavendish will see you,' she announced, with obvious disapproval in her tone. We went into a long, low-ceilinged room. At one end were French windows, the curtains of which were drawn back, with a glimpse beyond of the garden, gloomy in the mist and gathering dusk. By the open brick fireplace was a slim, attractive woman of about thirty-five. As the door closed behind us she came forward.

'Why have you come here?' she said, her voice low and tense.

Mr. Brett regarded her for a moment without answering. Then he said: 'You're in trouble, Mrs. Cavendish. I'm here to get you out of it — for a fee.'

She glanced at me, then at him. 'I am no longer in need of your help,' she said. And added unsteadily: 'Now.'

'You're sure of that?'

'Yes.'

'What — if you'll pardon the curiosity — has happened to make you change your mind? You didn't phone my office just to find out if a private detective sounds human.'

She drew a long, shuddering sigh. 'That danger no longer exists,' she said.

'That's something off your mind, then.' He paused. 'Only you don't sound so pleased. In fact, I would say you sound as if you have slipped out of the frying-pan into the fire.'

She stared at him intently. She said shakily: 'I had heard you were a very good detective, Mr. Brett, but I didn't realise you were so intuitively perceptive.'

He blew a ring of cigarette-smoke ceilingwards and watched it disintegrate. 'All of which adds up to what I told you: you're in trouble,' he murmured. 'Why don't you tell me about it?'

She said: 'I know you feel you're entitled to some sort of explanation. But I don't see how . . . ' She broke off. Then went on: 'When I telephoned you, it was because I was frightened for myself. Now, it's — it's someone else. As well.'

'You're talking,' he said. 'But you're not saying anything.'

Mrs. Cavendish turned towards me

appealingly. I gave her what I hoped was a smile of encouragement. 'Why not tell Mr. Brett,' I said. 'Whatever it is that's worrying you, even if it does concern someone else, Mr. Brett'll help you out.' It was the best I could think up. I was pretty sure he wasn't really concerned about her, though he was trying to give her that impression. The only thing bothering him was the fact he'd come all this way, and he didn't like the idea of making the trip for nothing.

Suddenly, he crossed to the door and jerked it open. He looked up and down the hall and, apparently satisfied no one was there, came back into the room, closing the door again. Mrs. Cavendish was looking at him with raised eyebrows. She said:

'Did you think someone might be listening?'

He smiled at her. 'That's what it looked like, didn't it? Who's this secretary-companion of yours?'

She said in some bewilderment: 'What are you suggesting? Surely you don't think she would . . . ?'

'I'm liable to think the worst of everybody: it's the way my mind works.' He shot her a long look. 'Does she know anything about — anything?'

Mrs. Cavendish shook her head emphatically. 'No, she definitely knows nothing.'

'How long has she been with you?'

'She joined us in South America. My husband was out there several years ago. Her name's Estella Cortez.'

'What about any other servants?'

'There's only my husband's manservant, who is away at the moment. And a cook-housekeeper, who lives out.'

Mr. Brett tapped the ash off his cigarette and contrived not to appear as irritable as I guessed he must be feeling. Mrs. Cavendish wasn't being at all helpful, and it looked as if it was going to take some hard spade-work to dig any information out of her. So far, it seemed he wasn't going to succeed in persuading her to hand him the job of straightening out her secret. But he didn't give up that easily. He said:

'You mentioned your husband, Mrs.

Cavendish. Where exactly does *he* figure in all this?'

There was an almost imperceptible pause before she answered. 'My husband?'

I noticed a faint narrowing of his eyes at the new note of apprehension that crept into her voice. But when he spoke, his voice was blandly casual. 'Yes.' He nodded. 'For a start, where is he now?'

'Here, of course,' she said. 'He's — he's probably reading in his study. He always reads until dinner.' She was talking quickly, as if she wanted to get away from the topic.

'Would it disturb him unduly if I had a chat with him?'

The effect of his laconically-put question was dramatic. Mrs. Cavendish looked sick, and swayed, so that I moved towards her. I thought she was going to pass out. But she pulled herself together.

'Will you please go?' she muttered. 'You *must* go — I order you to leave at once . . . '

Mr. Brett stared at her bleakly, without

moving. She picked up an expensive-looking leather handbag with a quick movement, so quick I imagined she was going to pull the old gun business on us. But what she drew out wasn't a gun — it was a wad of notes. I glanced at Mr. Brett and saw his expression brighten appreciably. She was saying:

'I realise I've caused you some trouble coming down here, Mr. Brett. Perhaps this will compensate you. I shouldn't have telephoned you — it was madness to do it. Please take this — and go. Go.'

Mr. Brett took the money, naturally. But he still made no attempt to go. 'If you'd care to add a further thirty to this,' he murmured as he pushed the notes into his wallet, 'I'd stay and clean up the whole business for you.' And added: 'Which would be cheaper than paying blackmail, anyway — there'll be no end to that.'

I gaped at him. *Blackmail!* I thought. How on earth did he know anything about that? Or was it just a shot in the dark? Whatever the answer on that score, there was no doubt about it having hit the bulls-eye — Mrs. Cavendish was looking at him as if he was something supernatural.

'*How — how did you know?*'

But he wasn't going to fool around replying to her questions even if he knew the answers, which he probably didn't. He pressed home the advantage he'd achieved by his last remark, snapping at her: 'Who is he? When are you seeing him again — tonight?'

She was wringing her hands agonisingly. 'I — I — I'll never see him again . . . '

'What d'you mean? If you'll never see him again, well, what's worrying you about that? Come on,' he urged her, 'come on, tell me. I'll put you right. I've told you that.'

'It's too late,' she said in a heavy voice. 'He's dead.'

Mr. Brett was drawing impatiently at his cigarette. Now he paused, exhaled slowly, and said through the cloud of smoke:

'Who killed him? You? Estella Whosit? Or could it be . . . ' His eyes had narrowed suddenly. ' . . . your husband interrupted his reading in his study to do the job?'

The tension in that room was so taut it almost twanged like a violin-string. I just stood there, staring first at Mr. Brett, then at the other. His long face jutted forward as if he was determined to drag the answers out of her. And then she caved in; just slumped into a chair, and began talking in a quiet voice.

'I was being blackmailed. He was coming again tonight for more money. I knew, of course, that when he'd got it he wouldn't leave me in peace for long. He'd want more . . . '

'That's the usual routine,' Mr. Brett said cheerfully.

'I had heard about you, and on the spur of the moment I decided to try and obtain your help. I wasn't expecting him for about an hour, and I thought if I could get you down here, you might do something . . . '

'You evidently believe I'm a fast worker.'

'I didn't know what I believed,' the

woman went on. 'I was crazy with worry and fear — the last few months have been a nightmare . . . '

'All right, Mrs. Cavendish; take it easy.'

She pulled herself together, then continued more steadily. 'And it was while I was on the phone that I heard him. He was out there — ' She glanced at the French windows. It was now almost dark outside. 'I rang off and went out to him. And then — then I saw he was in a state of collapse. There was blood . . . ' She buried her face in her hands as if to shut out the remembered horror. ' . . . he tried to say something, but I couldn't hear what it was. As I moved to steady him, he fell. He was dead . . . '

Mr. Brett said: 'Why do you think he had arrived earlier than you expected him?'

'I don't know.'

He indicated her to continue. 'Go on; what happened then?'

She said in a low voice: 'I — I dragged him across the lawn and left him behind the shrubbery. He was dead, I was sure of that. Nothing could be done for him, and

I was terrified my husband or Estella would arrive and find him.'

'It would have needed some explaining away,' Mr. Brett agreed, not without a certain dryness. But she wasn't listening. Still in that monotone, she went on:

'I came back here and tried to think what I should do. I asked myself who could have killed him. My husband? Had he . . . ?' She shuddered, then proceeded: 'You see, he's most terribly jealous and suspicious. It occurred to me he might have found out — about him, and . . . '

'If he'd killed him, he'd have come straight to you and told you, surely?' I asked.

She shook her head. 'Not necessarily. He might be waiting for me to go to him, confess that I was being blackmailed. And why. It would be like Guy to act like that. It's not that he's cruel, just that he would expect me to tell him first.'

'Why, instead of ringing me, didn't you go to the police?'

'I was afraid . . . '

'Scotland Yard would have taken care no one, not even your husband, would find out,' Mr. Brett said.

'I didn't know if I could be sure of that,' she murmured. 'You see, I'd written some letters to this man, and . . . '

'What was his name?'

'Harry Trannion.'

It occurred to me it was a difficult sort of name to remember. Automatically, I found myself saying the name over in my mind so I wouldn't forget it.

'You say he died without saying anything?' Mr. Brett went on. 'Gave you no idea who might have killed him?'

She shook her head mutely.

'Did you hear the sound of a shot?'

'No. He looked as if he'd been stabbed — in the back.'

Mr. Brett crushed his cigarette-stub into an ashtray thoughtfully. He turned to me. 'You stay with Mrs. Cavendish; I'll go and take a look at the late Mr. — '

He broke off and glanced at the French windows; there was a sudden curious scrabbling noise. I followed his look and heard the woman give a startled gasp:

'What was that . . . ?'

Her question was answered almost at

once, for the windows came open — she had obviously failed to close them properly — and something staggered drunkenly through them, before slowly making its way towards us.

'Harry!'

Mrs. Cavendish's cry was a mixture of horror and amazement.

The man was in a ghastly state: his clothes soaked and muddled; his hair lank across his face and smeared with blood. He halted and tried to pull himself fully upright, the effort drawing painful breaths from him. His mouth worked convulsively as he tried to speak . . . and then, as Mr. Brett moved towards him, the nightmarish figure suddenly gave a moan and pitched forward flat on his face.

Mr. Brett bent over him. After a cursory examination he stood up.

'He's dead now, anyway.' He turned to Mrs. Cavendish, who was staring in terror at the inert heap on the floor. 'Afraid your diagnosis was a trifle premature,' he said.

'But — but I thought . . . '

'He must've been only unconscious.'

'You mean, he came round,' I said, 'and

managed to stagger back here?' It seemed incredible.

He nodded. 'Pretty tough specimen.' He glanced down at the body. 'He was stabbed, all right. I wonder where the knife got to?' He gave a shrug and then nodded briskly at me. 'I think this is where you call the police.'

I hesitated a moment, glancing at Mrs. Cavendish, who was staring at the dead man. As I reached for the phone, she jerked her head up as if coming out of a trance.

'What are you going to do?'

I told her.

'But my husband . . . ' she burst out. 'They'll take my husband. Don't you understand?' She turned passionately to Mr. Brett. 'That's why I wanted you to go. I knew you'd bring the police in. I could have kept it quiet. I could have protected Guy . . . '

Mr. Brett's voice was like a lash. 'Get this, Mrs. Cavendish, and get it good: you can't shield anyone from *murder*. Not even your own husband. If he did it, he'll have to . . . '

'Have to do what?' a voice asked behind us.

Facing us in the doorway was a heavily-built man behind a double-barrelled shotgun. He came into the room and heeled the door shut.

'Guy . . . ' Mrs. Cavendish said, and started towards him.

'Keep to one side,' he told her; and she obeyed, watching him wide-eyed.

'Guy,' she pleaded, 'Mr. Brett came here to help me . . . '

'I understand perfectly,' he interrupted her brusquely, 'and am quite capable of taking care of the situation.' He gave Mr. Brett and myself what I interpreted as a distinctly unfriendly look, then he said to his wife: 'I think perhaps it would be better if you went.'

'But, Guy . . . '

'Please do as I ask.'

She looked helplessly at Mr. Brett and went out, closing the door behind her.

He came towards us purposefully.

Mr. Brett observed: 'Useful-looking fowling-piece you have.'

Guy Cavendish patted the breech

grimly. 'I'm sure you'll appreciate its bargaining power.'

'What are you trying to sell?'

Cavendish nodded at the body on the floor. 'My wife believes I killed this — blackmailer.' He saw Mr. Brett's eyebrows raised. 'Oh, yes, I overheard all that I needed to hear, though I have for some time suspected something was weighing on my wife's mind.' He went on: 'Whether you also believe me responsible for the creature's death, I don't know. What I do know is, you're not bringing any damned police here yet. You're getting out, both of you, and staying out.' He swung the gun threateningly in a half-circle. 'And the sooner the better — *for you*.'

Mr. Brett eyed him. 'If that's the way you feel about it,' he said gently, 'there's no object in our staying.'

'I'm gratified to learn you are a reasonable person.'

'It's a thing I hardly ever do — argue with a double-barrelled gun,' Mr. Brett said with engaging candour. 'Naturally,' he went on in agreeable tones, 'I'll go straight to the cops when I leave here.'

'I shouldn't expect you to do otherwise.'

Mr. Brett nodded. 'So long as we understand each other.'

I said, thinking maybe I might put in a word, 'Since we're all so friendly, couldn't you point that gun in some other direction?'

'I'm still telling you to get out,' he said unrelentingly. And kept a bead on us with that double-barrelled business. I shrugged and looked at Mr. Brett. As usual on these occasions, when I thought no good could come of staying, he was making no attempt to move. He was taking a lot of trouble tapping the ash off his cigarette into an ashtray on the writing-desk; then said, sounding as if he was really interested in the answer:

'What about our friend?' He gave a nod towards the man on the floor.

Cavendish glanced at the corpse. 'I intend to dispose of that in my own way.'

Did he, for his part, believe his wife had killed the man? It crossed my mind with a sudden light; if so, was his suspicion in fact entirely justified? Had Mrs. Cavendish been leading Mr. Brett up the garden path when she'd suggested her husband had taken care of the blackmailer? Had she seen a last desperate means of removing the menace to her peace of mind . . . ?

My growing conviction there might well be something in it was interrupted by the sudden appearance of more trouble in the person of Estella Cortez. She came into the room staring at Mr. Cavendish, who wheeled round at her — still keeping his gun threatening us.

'What do you want?' he rasped at her, moving in front of the body in an attempt to screen it from her view.

'But didn't you ring?'

He eyed her, opened his mouth to say something, then swung on Mr. Brett, his gaze travelling to the desk and — as I noticed for the first time — the bell-push that lay close to the ashtray.

Mr. Brett smiled at him, blandly. 'Must have touched it when I knocked off my cigarette-ash,' he said.

Livid, Cavendish stepped forward, only

to be brought up short by a cry from the woman. She was staring, her hand at her throat in horror, at the dead man.

Cavendish said bitterly: 'I meant to keep you out of this, but . . . ' He broke off and drew a deep breath as he realised the hopelessness of the situation, his shoulders suddenly bent with weariness. He turned a defeated expressed to Mr. Brent. 'All right. Go ahead, call the police.'

The Cortez woman was saying in a choked voice, 'But who — who is he?'

Mr. Brett said softly, 'Mrs. Cavendish may be able to identify him.'

The woman looked at him, at Cavendish. Then she seemed to grasp the significance of Mr. Brett's remark. 'You — you mean she . . . ?' she breathed.

There was a heavy silence.

Mr. Brett said, 'If you'll make up your mind to put that gun down, I'll phone.'

Cavendish looked stupidly at the weapon he was holding. The woman crossed to him quickly and, with a gentle firmness, took it, placing it out of harm's way. She seemed to have taken a grip of herself, though I fancied she averted her face from the body. Mr. Brett must have noticed it, too, because he waved me to the phone while he moved towards the dead man. 'Get it for me while I tidy up the place a trifle.'

'Yes, Mr. Brett,' I said. But before I could do anything about it, Estella Cortez had already reached the phone, and was saying almost briskly, 'I'll get them.'

Mr. Brett let her carry on with it and, taking up a light travelling-rug that was flung across a chair-back, spread it over the body. It looked prettier. I gave him a hand, heard the woman as she dialled suggest to Cavendish:

'Perhaps you'd like to see how Mrs. Cavendish is?'

He nodded, and with a look at Mr. Brett, who didn't stop him, went out. Mr. Brett crossed to the door watching after him. The woman said: 'I don't think he or his wife will try to run away.' She seemed to have recovered her composure and was the almost-dominating businesslike secretary I imagined her to be. But I spotted she was fiddling nervously with a pencil as she got through to the police number. Mr. Brett didn't answer her, only smiled bleakly and as he heard her say something into the mouthpiece moved from the door. 'I'll talk,' he said and took the receiver.

He gazed at the large blotting-pad as he talked to the police. 'Name of dead man is Trannion. It's murder, and I've got the killer all ready for you to collect.'

There was a sudden cold feeling under my scalp as I realised he was *staring straight at Estella Cortez.* She was quick in the uptake, too, but before she could do a thing about it he had moved and the double-barrelled gun was in his hands, pointing at her. He said softly: 'I think it's better in my hands than in yours.'

★ ★ ★

In a local bar some time later, Mr. Brett was explaining over a large Scotch. 'I had a hunch all along both Mrs. Cavendish and her husband could be ruled out.'

'Why?' I said. 'Personally, I'd had the

285

idea once or twice that she seemed guilty as could be.'

'Obviously she'd never have thought of getting me down here if she'd any idea of killing Trannion,' he said. 'So her story that she thought I could help her over the blackmail business, and then had found Trannion stabbed, made sense. It tied up with the way she broke off that phone call. Logical deduction from known facts.'

'I'll give you that,' I said.

'Thanks.'

'But what about the husband?'

'A man who's got a gun isn't going to mess about with a *knife*,' he said. 'He's the type who'd have blown Trannion to hell with both barrels, not skulked around a foggy garden getting his feet wet.'

I had to admit all this was sound enough reasoning, if not conclusive proof. I knew he'd trapped the Cortez woman, on the other hand, with proof that *had* been irrefutable. She'd broken down and made a statement when the police arrived; admitting her guilt, how she'd been working with the blackmailer (with whom she'd been infatuated), passing on the information about Mrs. Cavendish. Then, when Trannion threatened *her* with blackmail, she'd taken care of him. But what had given her away to Mr. Brett?

I asked him.

'She wrote it for me to read,' he said laconically.

I didn't get it. 'Wrote what when?'

He grinned at my obvious mystification. 'His name,' he said, 'while she was phoning the cops. Doodled it unconsciously on the blotting-pad.' I still hadn't caught on, and he said with an air of elaborate patience, 'She scribbled his name down — and just before, she'd been asking who he was. Remember?'

He saw by my face that the penny had dropped, and he muttered over his glass, 'I was wondering when it would sink in.'

I said, 'Pretty smart of you, Mr. Brett.'

He said, complacently, 'That's what I'm paid for, Gorgeous . . . '

'Especially,' I went on — and he eyed me warily, because I was laughing, 'as it was *I* who scrawled the name when

Mrs. Cavendish first told it to you. Tricky name to remember, so — perfect secretary — I made a note on the blotter!'

A Visitor at River Street

Tall and purposeful, Moberly loomed up out of the mist, his long overcoat flapping about his legs. At the gloomy-looking doorway he stopped to peer up and down River Street. No one passed him as he stood there, shivering a little in spite of his heavy coat. The fog made an almost impenetrable shroud, through which a street lamp contrived to glimmer a watery yellow. The night was raw and chilly, but it was not that which brought the cold, sick sensation to the pit of his stomach.

For a full minute he remained motionless, shoulders hunched, hands thrust deep into his pockets; listening, straining his ears to make sure his arrival had not been witnessed. The little street appeared deserted. As if from another world, a taxi hooted once or twice, and a car purred along the waterfront. From the river came the muffled, eerie note of the siren as a tug groped her way through the fog.

Satisfied he was unobserved, he slipped through the half-open door and quickly crossed to the dimly-lit stairway curving to his uncle's rooms. The mist swirled and threw strange shadows across the walls, grotesquely patched where the paint had peeled, the plaster fallen away. The dank smell rising from the stone floor struck sharply at his nostrils. Suddenly he felt something brush against his ankles. He stopped with a muttered exclamation. A pair of eyes glimmered up at him from the gloom.

'Blasted cat!' And Moberly shoved it aside with his foot. It crouched against the wall, its eyes following him as he went cautiously up the stairs. They were slippery and treacherous in the darkness. And tonight there must be no stumbling.

The previous night, he had called on his uncle as the result of a rare invitation the old man had extended him. Though they had little enough in common, Moberly had gone with the idea that Uncle Luke's garrulity might distract him for a while. And he needed distraction. The strain was beginning to tell. Embezzlement was an ugly business, and unless he got money damnably quick he was for it. When he had left Uncle Luke a little later, he was trembling so that he had found it difficult to light his cigarette. There, in that very room, was a means of escape from the trap that was closing on him.

Halfway up the stairs Moberly paused in his grim, unhesitating ascent to crush the rising agitation of blood and nerves. He tried to make himself believe his pounding heartbeats were saying: 'It's not murder!' — It's *not* murder!'

Now he started up the steps again. His mouth was a thin line, eyes hard and glittering in the shadow of his hat.

A few minutes later he was saying, 'Hope you'll forgive my butting in on you like this, Uncle. Only my friend is so keen to know all about this idol — er — god, or whatever it is.'

'It is a goddess, my boy.'

'Beg her pardon!' Moberly's mouth twisted into a smile. 'You see, my pal's going away tomorrow. As a matter of fact, he wanted to come along and have a chat with you before he went. I thought you might not like that, but if you could tell me the yarn over again, I'll pass it on to him.'

'You say he's a journalist, this friend of yours?'

Moberly nodded. 'We lunched together today, and I happened to mention the story about your — er — goddess. I couldn't remember much to tell him, but he was tremendously interested. Said it would fit in with some magazine articles he is planning.'

The old man snorted indignantly. 'I suppose what he's after is to pick my brains, dig this story from me second-hand, so to speak, furbish it up and sell it as his own effort!'

Moberly cursed inwardly. The tale he had invented to explain away his second visit had merely succeeded in putting the old fool's back up. He said hurriedly, 'I'm sure he'd be glad to compensate you — '

'Bosh! Nonsense!' The other waved the suggestion away.

'He's an awfully decent type, Uncle,' Moberly said. 'I mean, he does know what he's writing about, really. This particular story's taken his fancy, and he'd be enormously grateful to you if you'd help him.'

'Well, I don't approve of his methods. However . . . What is it you want to know?' Uncle Luke eyed him over the top of his spectacles.

Moberly found it difficult to restrain a great sigh of relief. He swallowed, then smiled with a studied mixture of apology and gratitude.

'If you could just go over the story as you told it me last night.'

'Hmmm . . . I think the best thing would be for me to read you Crowther's letter.' His uncle rose from his chair. The movement caused him to wheeze, coughing raspingly. 'Curse this vile fog!' he choked through the paroxysm.

Moberly watched his face grey as he fought for breath. Useless old fossil! He had one foot in the grave already. Might kick the bucket any minute. His heart was very weak. Why shouldn't he snuff out that fitful flame? he asked himself. *Now*, when it would benefit him?

He stood up, and his eyes left the other to take in the shabby room cluttered with books and curios. There was no reason why Uncle Luke should live in this lonely dinginess. He could well afford more comfortable and pleasant surroundings if he chose. His eccentric parsimony alone made him exist as he did. Only stupid sentimentalists could say it was a crime to remove this futile, dried-up husk of senility.

Moberly's gaze came to rest on the figure in the corner of the room.

About eighteen inches high, it stood amidst a litter of oddities on the sideboard. The light from the gas lamp did not reach it, so that it made a dark, squat mass there. But it wore a strange suggestion of life that was a little sinister. Its eyes added to its quiescent animation. Aslant in the round features, made of some coppery substance, they caught the light and held it. Like the eyes of a cat seen in the dark. From the centre of the figure came a warm, blood-red glow, glimmering with wondrous depth and quality. Moberly knew well the source of that flickering gleam. Six rubies set in the gold hilt of a miniature sword which was driven into the figure's breast. He stared across the room, fascinated.

'The Goddess of the Sword of Vengeance.'

His uncle's rasping voice broke into his thoughts. In his momentary preoccupation he had forgotten the old man. He forced a casualness into his tone as he turned to him.

'Queer piece of work! Don't know that I quite go for her.'

Uncle Luke adjusted his spectacles which his fit of coughing had knocked askew.

'She won't harm you if you treat her with the proper respect she deserves. But anger her, and she'll show her annoyance in no unmistakable fashion!'

Moberly's thin lips curved in an indulgent smile.

'You may grin, young man, as others grinned! When you're as old as I, you'll learn to be somewhat less sceptical.'

'I don't know that I'm sceptical, Uncle. I just don't see how an inanimate object like your goddess can do either harm or good.'

'I won't waste my time trying to convince you. And, by the way, she doesn't belong to me. She's Crowther's property. Now, where's the letter?'

The old man made his way to his desk, and fumbled among the papers and books which crowded it. Presently, wheezing and muttering, he dragged forth a piece of paper with an exclamation of triumph.

'This is it, I think. Yes . . . Let's bring it near the light.' He lowered himself into a battered old armchair underneath the lamp and peered short-sightedly at the letter in his shaking fingers. Moberly leant against the table just behind him. Among the odds and ends on there lay a heavy brass candlestick. Uncle Luke twisted to look up at him.

'Sit down, my boy, sit down,' he muttered irritably. 'Might as well be comfortable while you listen to this.'

'I'm comfortable enough, thanks, Uncle.'

'As you please, as you please.' And the

old man leaned forward to read. Cautiously, Moberly slid his right hand along the table. Unobtrusively he leaned back until he touched the candlestick.

" . . . I came across the goddess in an old temple in a little island just off Bali', his uncle read. "I bribed a priest to let me have it; which he did, on condition I did not carry it about with me, but dispatched it to England immediately. He was afraid it might be discovered by someone and its loss traced back to him.

"Thought you might like to take care of it for me until I got back. I know it will amuse you to have around your 'museum', and also, if anything should happen to me, I'd like you to have it.

"One thing, however, I do beg you to remember. The sword driven into the figure (the hilt is, you will perceive, studded with six very fine rubies) is moveable. *But on no account remove it!*

"It is a long story, one I hope to regale you with when we meet. But the gist is that the idol represents an age-old goddess who was slain by a jealous lover possessed of a magic sword. Before she died, she laid a curse on anyone who should draw the sword out of her body. Her idea being, I suppose, that her hasty lover should do no more harm with it. The curse of the goddess was to the effect that anyone defying her would die, and by their own hand.

"'The idol is a miniature replica of the goddess, and is worshipped as the 'Goddess of the Sword of Vengeance' — rough translation of the Javanese — and the curse is still carried on through it in all its deadliness. This may read as awful nonsense, no doubt, but to my knowledge two men who removed the sword, though it was subsequently returned, died — *and by their own hands*. One committed suicide. The other killed himself accidentally. Believe me, sceptic as I am, I wouldn't pull out that sword for anything! And I want you to take the greatest care that neither you nor anybody else ever does so.

"'Next week I leave for Sumatra, where . . . ''

Uncle Luke laid down the letter.

'There you have the story, my boy.' He

turned and blinked up at the other. 'I hope — ' he began, but the rest of the sentence was strangled in his throat.

Moberly struck once.

Uncle Luke gave a little groan and fell back quietly into his chair. His head lolled forward on his chest and a thin trickle — almost black, it seemed, against the white skin — began to ooze from the wound on his temple.

Moberly stood bent and rigid against the table, his breath escaping through clenched teeth in a long hiss. He stared, as if with uncomprehending astonishment, at the blood which ran over the closed eyelid and dripped on to the cheek. A moment of panic seized him. He opened his mouth to utter a cry of horror. No words came, merely a choked gurgle, then he pulled himself together. He had done what he had set out to do. No turning back now.

He let the candlestick fall on to the table, and the action simultaneously drove the last remnants of panic away. An icy calm flooded his brain, took possession of him. He saw everything very clearly. He moved with a deliberate precision.

First, he carefully wiped the candlestick with his handkerchief. Then he turned to his uncle and lifted him from the chair. Holding him upright, he placed his ear against his heart. He was dead. Satisfied of that, he let him slump to the floor so that his head rested on the sharp angle of the iron kerb. He held the old man's spectacles shoulder-high and dropped them on to the hearth. The letter, he picked up and placed in his inside pocket.

He eyed the body for a moment or two, adjusted its position a little. Turned the head more to one side, drew one leg up slightly. At last he was convinced no one would think twice about the cause of death. The old man had been overcome with a heart attack, had collapsed, fallen and struck his head.

Moberly smiled thinly to himself. He advanced towards the corner to face the goddess; and, as if she were indeed a living thing, as if the slant eyes in the inscrutable countenance were not those of a dead image but of a creature of flesh and blood, he gave it back stare for stare.

For a long moment he gazed at her. Then, with a soft laugh, stretched forth his hand to pluck the sword. It came away from the body easily and he held it up to the light. The blade was about six inches long and half an inch wide. It was beautifully fashioned of steel, with a delicately-worked design decorating each side. But it was the hilt which made him catch his breath. The rubies glowed with a rich, exquisite beauty as he twirled the blade slowly round between thumb and finger. He wrapped the sword in his handkerchief and, as he did, the point pricked him and he made a wry face.

'No rose without its thorn!' he murmured, and slipped his prize into the same pocket that held the letter.

He crossed swiftly to the door, gave the room a last searching look, and went out.

As he reached the bottom of the slippery stairway, there was a quick movement at his feet, and he only just saved himself from pitching headlong. It was the cat which had darted across his path.

River Street was as empty as it had been when he arrived. The fog was beginning to lift, and a little while later he hailed a taxi. He gave the man his address and told him to hurry.

He lay back in the taxi and for the first time allowed his tensed muscles to relax. He made an effort to analyse his emotions. He had expected some sort of subtle but significant change to have taken place within him. But he felt nothing. Only a triumphant relief.

He lit a cigarette, savoured the exhilaration which enveloped him. He felt as if he had taken some marvellous drug. A tremendous sense of power gripped him.

After a moment, he drew the handker-chief from his pocket and unwrapped it. Leaning forward so that it caught the light from the street lamps, he held the sword and twisted it over and over between his fingers. The hilt winked back at him.

There came a sudden screeching of brakes. A frightful jerk catapulted Moberly from his seat. He grabbed the hilt desperately, fearful the sword would slip and be crushed underfoot. He did not loosen his grip as he fell helplessly forward, the point turned towards him.

'Sorry, sir,' the taxi driver apologized cheerfully, pulling open the door. 'Nasty skid! 'Ope it didn't shake yer up!'

No reply.

The driver felt for the switch.

'Cor, fainted!' he muttered as the light revealed the inert figure. He ducked into the taxi and turned Moberly over onto his back. It was then he saw the jewelled hilt sticking from his chest.

'Cripes!' he grunted. 'Blinkin' suicide, eh?'

Mr. Walker Sees the Show

'If you arsks *me*,' said Mr. Walker, lifting his glass and examining its contents with a critical eye, 'there ain't nothink like a good comedian.' Whereupon he proceeded to lower a portion of beer down his throat.

This praiseworthy object achieved, he smacked his lips, subjected the now half-empty glass to a momentary reflection, and replaced it on the bar counter.

The landlord of the Royal Duke nodded. 'Yes, an 'earty laugh when you're feelin' down in the dumps is as good as a tonic. Like that Billy Bennett, now. Scream, he is.'

'S'right.' And Mr. Walker drew the back of his hand across his mouth. 'Single-'anded tonight, chum?' he observed.

'Yes; it's Arthur's night off. Always the way when we're busy.'

'S'right.'

Leaning on an elbow, he glanced round

309

the crowded bar. Most of the customers were enjoying a quick one before hurrying over to the Coronet Music Hall across the street, where the first house was shortly to begin.

His gaze rested on a young woman nearby who was holding an animated conversation with two men. The garish light caught at her tawny hair, and there was the glitter of rings on the scarlet-nailed hand that clasped her drink.

'Across the way, she is,' the landlord breathed hoarsely in his ear.

'Oh, ah?'

'Yes; she's the one what the feller throws knives at.'

'Yer mean Mexican Pete and Rosita?' Mr. Walker had seen the names on a poster outside the music hall. He had been suitably impressed by the gaudy illustration of a dark man in a Mexican sombrero and bell-bottomed trousers about to hurl a dagger at a girl, who wore little more than a nonchalant smile as she stood with other daggers stuck perilously around her.

'Saw 'em the other night,' the man

behind the bar went on. 'Good, too. Fair miracle the way he slings them knives about. Just misses her by an 'air's-breadth every time. She's a tough 'un all right.' And added: 'They say she's a flighty bit o' goods, too.'

Rosita was laughing loudly at some remark made by one of her companions, clutching at the other man's arm in her paroxysm of mirth.

Mr. Walker found an infectious quality in her laughter and could not restrain an involuntary chuckle. As he watched her, she gave a sudden glance up at the clock and quickly emptied her glass. With a word to the two men, she left them and hurried out.

'Been in every evenin' this week, she has,' said the landlord, and added with a wink, 'Arthur'll be sorry he missed her. Got an eye for pretty girls, has Arthur. You should see him when he's s'posed to be cleanin' my front steps — half the time he's watchin' the chorus girls in and out of the stage door.'

Mr. Walker chuckled throatily. 'Yes, when I was passin' with me barrer this mornin', I saw 'im — one eye on 'is job and the other across the street, like. Ah, well — we was all young once.' And he reached for his beer.

A short while later found him leaning inquiringly through the cubby-hole inside the Coronet stage door. The doorkeeper regarded him with a dubious face.

'Dunno as I can let you through tonight,' he said. 'Things is a bit 'umpy.'

'What's wrong, Charlie?'

'It's this Mexican Pete — '

'I seen his partner across the pub just now.'

'It's her what's causin' all the trouble. Oh, she don't mean no harm, I don't suppose. But with him bein' so jealous, and her carryin' on a flirtation with Eddie Davis — you know, the stage manager — '

Mr. Walker nodded; and the other, after glancing right and left, lowered his voice confidentially. 'Mexican Pete's sweet on her, an' keeps throwin' jealously fits — '

'Well, s'long as 'e don't throw no knives about!'

'Shouldn't wonder — *wot* a vi'lent

temper he's got! Anyway, Eddie's kind of sniffy hisself, and liable to flare up at anythin' out of the way.'

'I gets yer, chum.'

Charlie suddenly opened his mouth as a thought struck him. 'Tell you what, though,' he said, 'even if it would be risky sneaking you in to watch from the wings . . . you'd be all right up in the flies. You know, where they lowers the scenery from.'

The junk man's rubicund face brightened. 'Bird's-eye view, eh?'

'How'd that suit you?'

'Anythink to oblige, chum, that's me all over,' was the response.

Charlie led the way up a flight of stone steps which ascended to and past the dressing rooms. As they neared one of the rooms they heard the sound of angry voices from within. A voice with a pronounced foreign accent was making the most row.

'That's him!' muttered the stage door keeper.

'I tella you, I not put up with it! I not letta you spik to 'eem!' Mexican Pete was shouting. And then came Rosita's voice, more subdued and rather bored. 'Oh, shut up! I'm speaking to who I like. You can't order me about — '

'I killa heem! I killa you!'

'Lumme!' gulped Mr. Walker as he and Charlie paused outside the door.

'You're crazy jealous,' the girl was saying. 'You talk as if we're married — '

'So we will be!'

'Well, until that happy day, I'll talk to all the men I take a fancy to!'

At this, the knife thrower seemed to lose all control. His voice reached a screech. 'If you spika to thisa fella again, I — I *make a mistake wit' a knife!*'

Rosita's answer was almost as explosive. 'Get out! Get out of my room!'

Charlie tugged at Mr. Walker's elbow. 'Come on! He'll be comin' out — '

The junk man followed him, shaking his head, and the door handle of Rosita's room rattled as Pete started to make his exit. Mr. Walker caught the last words of their altercation.

'I go. But I 'ave warned you — '

'That's it, stupid,' she mocked him.

'Cut off my ear and spoil the act!'

Charlie pulled open an iron door that opened onto a dark tangle of ropes and scenery and the blare of a dance band that was performing on the stage below. He led the way across to a wooden rail which was the only separation from the platform they were traversing and a sheer drop to the stage.

'Not that I reckon he would,' muttered Charlie.

''Oo would what?' grunted Mr. Walker, as he narrowly missed sprawling over a coil of rope. His companion turned.

'Why, Pete, o' course. He wouldn't let one of his daggers slip like he said he would.'

'Glad to 'ear it,' returned the junk man. But there was doubt in his voice.

'No,' said the other. 'You see, he's an *artiste* — and artistes never thinks of nothing but their show. See? Too proud, they are. I've heard Mexican Pete boast as how he's never had an accident in the whole of his career. Think he'd ruin hisself just out of jealousy?'

'Well, I — ' Mr. Walker hesitated.

'Not likely. 'Course, when you hears him lettin' off steam like he was just now, you feels as if he really would do something murderous — even I've felt it for a while — but when you adds it up . . . no. Like I said, he's too much of an artist. See?'

Mr. Walker nodded, blew out his round cheeks with relief.

'You're right, Charlie. Why, that's these people's motto, ain't it? 'The Show Must Go On'.'

'S' the idea. Well, I'm hoppin' back now, or I'll get the sack. After this band is Mexican Pete and then a comedian.'

The junk man pushed his bowler hat onto the back of his head and, leaning his bulk gingerly on the rail, looked down upon the activity below.

The band was reaching the climax of its act, and Mr. Walker could see the stagehands in the wings waiting in readiness to change the setting for the act that was to follow. It was then he saw Rosita with her arm round Eddie Davis's neck and smiling up into his face. As he watched, he saw her pull his head down and whisper something, and then both of them laughed.

Mr. Walker's face grew troubled as he looked down at them. What a fool the girl was, he thought, for she was blatantly the one who was making all the advances. Supposing Mexican Pete were to see her?

In spite of Charlie's argument, the junk man reckoned, there would be trouble with a capital T for her, and no mistake. He for one wouldn't pin too much faith in such circumstances that the knife thrower wouldn't forget his artistic pride. Blood would flow . . .

A movement a few feet away caused him to turn his head. It was Mexican Pete.

The knife thrower was staring down at the stage, his face contorted with jealous fury. Mr. Walker felt an icy chill run down his spine as he caught that twisted look. Hidden as he was by a number of ropes running from overhead, and the darkness, Pete had not seen him. As he watched, he heard the final blare of the dance band and the crash of applause. The other turned away and, mouthing to himself, hurried off.

'I killa *her* — I killa *her* — '

Mr. Walker saw him disappear through the iron door, and mopped his moist brow with his handkerchief. 'Lumme,' he muttered, ''ere's a nice 'ow-d'yer-do!'

Mexican Pete bowed to the applause and showed his white teeth in a smile.

'And now, ladies and gen'l'mans — I come to my most deefcult treeck. You see Rosita over t'ere — and 'ere I 'ave twelve daggers. T'ese I will t'row one by one een such a way t'ey will, wit'out touching 'er, 'old 'er firmly to the board against which she is now standing — ah!' He gave an exclamation under his breath as one of the knives he was holding slipped to the floor.

'S'fust time I ever see 'im drop one.'

It was one of the men working in the flies who muttered the remark into Mr. Walker's ear as they looked down at the stage. The junk man was breathing heavily, and was forced continually to mop his face and run the handkerchief round his limp collar.

His first impulse had been to chase

318

after the knife thrower in the vague hope that he might be able to prevent the tragedy he felt convinced was to take place upon the brilliantly lit stage. But he realized he was powerless.

He would never be able to find his way to the stage before Mexican Pete's act was in progress, when it would be too late. It would be futile to try and stop the performance: no one would pay much, if any, attention to him. Everybody was too used to the knife thrower's jealous outbursts to pay much attention to them.

And so he remained among the ropes and scenery, and in sweating apprehension watched Mexican Pete and Rosita go through the routine of their act. He tried to persuade himself that he was making a fuss about nothing. That Charlie's ideas about the knife thrower were right. But he couldn't forget Pete's face, his murderously whispered words: 'I killa *her* — '

Now his voice came up to him.

'Ladies and gen'l'mans — I t'row the first dagger!'

From his gloved hand the knife flew, to stick quivering, perilously close to the white figure posed against the black, velvet-covered board. Above the roll of the orchestra drums came the audience's gasp, sibilant and ending in a sigh of relief.

'I t'row the second dagger!'

Mr. Walker's heart was a sledge-hammer beating in his chest.

He was only conscious that it was all over when he saw Mexican Pete and Rosita smiling and bowing over the footlights, and the applause of the audience reaching him like the roar of the sea. He staggered away from the rail and subsided on an upturned box, fanning himself with his bowler hat.

'Thank 'eavens! Charlie was right, arter all,' he kept repeating to himself. He began to grin sheepishly as he realised the panic he'd got into over nothing at all.

'Lumme,' he decided after a moment or two, 'a nice drop o' beer wouldn't come amiss, arter all that!'

A little way past Rosita's dressing room, he kicked against something; bending to pick it up, he saw that it was a circular rubber heel. It was very worn, but the junk man believed in wasting nothing, and slipped it into his pocket.

As he did so Rosita herself hurried up the steps, passed him with a friendly smile, and left him slightly dizzy from her perfume. When his head cleared it occurred to him that she must have remained behind some time after her act had finished. Flirting with the stage manager again, he supposed.

Ah well, he reassured himself, she'd grow out of her foolishness all in good time. Settle down and many Mexican Pete, most likely. And, chuckling, Mr. Walker went on down.

★   ★   ★

Hurrying into her dressing room, Rosita started to close the door while she felt for the switch, when a hand came out of the darkness and grabbed her wrist. She opened her mouth to scream; but another hand, also gloved, was clapped over it, and the door slammed behind her.

★   ★   ★

'So the police think 'e's done it, eh?' asked Mr. Walker. Charlie nodded glumly. It was the following morning, and the junk man had read in a newspaper of the murder of Rosita in her dressing room.

He had also read that Mexican Pete had been detained by the police. The news had stunned Mr. Walker, and he had quickly made his way to the Coronet stage door in search of fuller details of the murder from Charlie.

'Must've been just after you'd gone,' said the doorkeeper. 'Eddie Davis goes up to her room to have a drink with her, and finds the light out and her dead — strangled. Awful-lookin', she was, poor thing. Well, then the police is here, you know, asking everyone questions and pokin' their noses all over the place.

'Anyway, the upshot of it all is, they takes Mexican Pete — they found him havin' a drink in the stage bar — along with 'em. Detained for questionin', they calls it. Poor devil! He looked knocked all of a heap. 'I didn't do it, I didn't do it,' he kept saying. And I don't reckon he did.' Then Charlie added dejectedly, 'Though who else it was, I can't think.'

Mr. Walker pursed his lips. 'Looks bad for 'im, does it?' he asked, quietly.

'Well, he was always threatenin' her. You know, like we heard him last night — by the way, I didn't say nothing about you bein' up there, could cost me my job — '

'Trust me, chum.'

'All the same,' continued Charlie, 'you'd have thought if he'd wanted to kill her he'd have done it accidental-like, during the act. He'd have got away with it then, easy.'

Mr. Walker nodded. He recalled the harrowing moments he had spent the night before. 'But your idea was, he was too much of an artist,' he said. 'And I reckons you was right,' he added.

'I know.'

'Did the police find any clues what they could sorter pin on 'im?'

'Only that there wasn't no fingerprints on her neck, which proved the murderer must have wore gloves — and Pete wears 'em, part of his costume.'

'S'right enough.'

'Then there wasn't nothing stolen, though there was enough jewellery lying about. So it didn't look like a thief had done it. Besides, how could anyone have got in? No one who I didn't know came through here last night.'

''Ow about when you was up over the stage with me?'

'I thought of that. I wasn't away more than five minutes, and when I got back here, I found the call boy keepin' me seat warm for me. He hadn't seen no strangers go through. Besides, even if someone had got in, he couldn't have got out without me seein' him.'

'That's true.' And Mr. Walker shook his head sadly. 'Lumme, it looks like it couldn't 'ave been nobody but 'im, don't it, mate?'

'It do.'

'And yet — ' began the junk man, then checked himself. 'Ah, well, we'll see, I s'pose.' He shifted himself from the cubby-hole against which he had been leaning. 'Better be gettin' along, Charlie,' he said. 'See you later, I shouldn't wonder.' And he ambled off.

An hour later, his rotund figure overflowed the chair in which he sat opposite Detective Inspector Wedge in his office at Scotland Yard. The latter moved his long cigarette holder from one side of his mouth to the other, and said through the cloud of tobacco smoke:

'But surely, if your theory's right, doesn't it point to his guilt rather than his innocence?'

Mr. Walker held his bowler hat more firmly on his knee and leant forward. 'That's 'ow it looked to me,' he said hoarsely, then added, '*at first*.' He paused significantly. 'But workin' it out logically to its final — 'ow d'yer call it? — conclusion, it don't. You agrees as 'ow Mexican Pete didn't murder 'er durin' the show, because it would spoil 'is act, and 'e was very proud of hisself as an artiste?'

Inspector Wedge nodded in agreement.

'Well, for that very same reason, 'e wouldn't *never* try and kill 'er — off the stage nor on.' Mr. Walker's voice shook a little and became more throaty in his excitement. 'Don't you see? She meant too much to 'is act for 'im to want to lose 'er. 'E'd found 'er and trained 'er to stand up all noncherlant while 'e slung them daggers at 'er.

'Now, you don't find pretty girls what 'ave got the nerve to do that everywhere. 'Owever 'e may've felt about 'er carryings-on with other blokes, 'owever jealous 'e was — she was a perfect partner for 'im on the stage. And for 'im, 'is show comes before everythink. Everythink.

'Lumme, look at the mess 'e's in now. 'Is bread and butter's gorn down the drain, smack. It'll take 'im months before 'e'll find a girl like poor Rosita, and train 'er so's she's as good as she was.'

Inspector Wedge's sardonic features relaxed in a thin smile. He had known the junk man for a long time, and had reason to respect his shrewd intelligence and insight into the characters of the various people with whom he came into contact.

There was certainly a well of truth in his reasoning in this particular case. He had presented quite a fresh angle to it which the inspector was forced to admit

326

had not occurred to him. He crushed out the stub from his cigarette holder and fitted a fresh cigarette into it. He leaned back in his chair and thoughtfully puffed a cloud of smoke upwards.

'Any idea who *did* do it?' he asked quietly.

Mr. Walker looked at him, pulling at his fat jowl. He hesitated appreciably before he answered. 'I dunno,' he said, and sighed heavily. The detective sat up with a jerk, his eyes narrowed.

'Who is it?'

The other rose from his chair and gave an embarrassed cough. 'I'll be gettin' along, chum,' he muttered. 'I'm glad you thinks there's somethink in what I've told you. I'll — er — I'll be seein' you later, I shouldn't wonder.'

★ ★ ★

'He's only just come in,' the woman told him, as Mr. Walker stepped into the dingy hall. 'He'll be having his tea,' she said, closing the front door. He ambled after her and she knocked at the door of a room at the back. 'A visitor for you,' she called out, and turned the handle. The junk man went in.

'Good evenin', chum,' he said. 'Sorry to pop in on you like this.'

'Bit of a surprise, I must say,' was the answer. 'I didn't expect — oh well, what d'you want, anyway?'

'Thought we might 'ave a cosy little chat, you and me — now, don't let me interrupt your tea. I'll take the weight off me feet, if you don't mind, and smoke me pipe.'

'Go ahead.'

'Thanks, mate.' And Mr. Walker lowered himself slowly into a decrepit armchair before a fire that burned fitfully in the grate. The other watched him, stirring his tea mechanically as his visitor fumbled for his pipe. He lit up and sucked noisily at it, and then observed: 'You know, there ain't nothink like a good 'eart-to-'eart — it 'elps to clear the air, like.'

'What makes you think I'd have anything to talk to you about?'

'Oh, just a sort of feelin' I got, that's

all. But you don't 'ave to worry about doin' any chin-waggin', yours truly can take care o' that. That is, if you don't mind listenin'?'

The other was silent. Mr. Walker regarded him with an almost sorrowful expression, and saw him nervously cross and uncross his legs.

'It must be an awful thing,' he said, 'to be accused of a crime what you ain't never done. And I reckons too as 'ow it can't be very 'appy for the other bloke, the one what *as* done it, knowin' an innercent person is goin' to suffer for 'im.' He paused to apply another match to his pipe, then went on: 'F'rinstance, think what a murderer must go through, lyin' in bed of a night and thinking someone else is goin' to get 'ung for 'is crime. 'E must find easy, restful sleep 'ard to come by, I reckons, don't you?'

No reply.

'And o' course it must be even worse for 'im if he does actually *let* that other bloke swing for 'im. Worse even than bein' 'ung, I should say. Knowin' 'e'll 'ave to go the rest of 'is life . . . 'aunted. Yes, 'aunted.' Mr. Walker shook his head slowly. 'Lumme,' he said, 'I'd rather own up and face the music, I would, even if it meant — '

'How did you know?' the other suddenly broke in.

The junk man looked at him. He bent and tapped his pipe against the grate, then heaved himself to his feet. He fumbled in his pocket and put something on the table.

'It was outside 'er dressin' room last night,' he said, indicating the circular rubber heel. Involuntarily, the other man glanced at his foot, and then checked himself. Mr. Walker eyed him mournfully. 'It's off your right 'eel. Came off last night.' His voice was gentle. 'It was 'er jewellery you was after, but she came in and surprised you, so you killed 'er. You was too frightened to take anythin' then — '

'This heel doesn't prove a thing. I could've lost it up there the night before — '

'If you 'ad, the cleaners would 'ave swept it up. They does the passages and

330

stairs every mornin'. Besides, I seen it on your boot yesterday — '

'When?'

'When you was cleanin' the steps. Remember, I passed you? And this mornin', when I comes by again, I 'appens to notice 'ow it was missin'. I didn't think of it till later — Charlie said somethink about you passin' 'im at the stage door, just about the time o' the murder, with a tray and glasses.

'Clever of you, that was. You knew people was used to you 'oppin' in and out with drinks for the performers, and it wouldn't strike anyone to mention you to the police. That's what you counted on last night. And it would 'ave come off, too — only I remembered *you wasn't supposed to be on duty last night*, and then I remembers that.' He indicated the rubber heel.

There was silence in the room.

'Well, Arthur?' Mr. Walker's voice was husky, a whisper.

'All right, then — I'll tell the police. Will you come with me?'

They went along together.

We do hope that you have enjoyed reading this large print book.

Did you know that all of our titles are available for purchase?

We publish a wide range of high quality large print books including:
Romances, Mysteries, Classics
General Fiction
Non Fiction and Westerns

Special interest titles available in large print are:
The Little Oxford Dictionary
Music Book, Song Book
Hymn Book, Service Book

Also available from us courtesy of Oxford University Press:
Young Readers' Dictionary
(large print edition)
Young Readers' Thesaurus
(large print edition)

For further information or a free brochure, please contact us at:
Ulverscroft Large Print Books Ltd.,
The Green, Bradgate Road, Anstey,
Leicester, LE7 7FU, England.
Tel: (00 44) **0116 236 4325**
Fax: (00 44) **0116 234 0205**

Other titles in the
Linford Mystery Library:

THE RED TAPE MURDERS

Gerald Verner

Superintendent Budd's latest murder investigation begins with the murder of a solicitor, found strangled with red tape. Soon, two more local solicitors are murdered in similar fashion. Eventually Budd learns that two years earlier, a man shot himself when about to lose the bungalow he built, under a compulsory purchase order of the council. Two of the solicitors had acted in the sale of the land, and the third had acted for the council. Is someone seeking vengeance for the man who committed suicide — himself a victim of red tape?

REDEMPTION TRAIL

Victor Rousseau

Petty criminal Alfred Collins finds himself the victim of a conspiracy to frame him for murder. Sentenced to twenty years in prison, he manages to effect a daring escape, and assumes a new identity. Eventually he learns that the man who framed him has fled to work for a lumbering company. Consumed with the passion for revenge and the thought of being able to force a confession that would clear his name and free him from the life of a fugitive, Collins follows his trail into the Canadian wilderness . . .